Little Songs in the Shade of Tamaara

little songs
in the shade
of tamaara

MOHAMMED AFIFI

Translated by Lisa White

The University of Arkansas Press
Fayetteville
2000

Originally published with the title *Taraniim fii Dhill Tamaara.*

04   03   02   01   00   5   4   3   2   1

Designed by Liz Lester

⊗   The paper used in this publication meets the minimum requirements of the American National Standard for Permanence of Paper
for Printed Library Materials Z39.48-1984.

Library of Congress Cataloging-in-Publication Data

'Afīfī, Muḥammad, 1922–1981.
[Tarānīm fī ẓill Tamārā. English]
Little songs in the shade of Tamaara / Mohammed Afifi ;
translated by Lisa White.
p.   cm.
ISBN 1-55728-614-0 (pbk.)
I. White, Lisa, 1954–   . II. Title.
PJ7810.F519T3713 2000
892.7'36—dc21   00-010353

Acknowledgments

While at work on this project, I was fortunate to have the encouragement of a number of friends and colleagues, not to mention the generous support of the Near Eastern Studies Department of Cornell University, which provided travel expenses for a trip to Cairo for the summer of 1998, when much more than I realized was yet to be done.

I am forever indebted to the most cosmopolitan of godmothers, Kate Barcus Harris, whose gift so many years ago of a wonderful dictionary first made me think seriously of a career in foreign languages. Her unflagging enthusiasm for all my endeavors has ever since been a source of wonder to me.

I also thank Mahmoud Albatal, the first to urge me to consider entering the University of Arkansas translation competition and Marilyn Booth for her good advice. I am particularly grateful to Bill Granara for his very helpful critique of the first draft, to Brian King, my insightful editor, and to Margaret Larkin for her valuable suggestions and unwavering moral support in the trying days of the final revisions.

Contents

Translator's Introduction

A noted member of Nobel laureate Naguib Mahfouz's circle, Al-Harafiish, Mohammed Afifi was dubbed "the satirist." One of four children, he was born on February 25, 1922, in the small delta town of Zifta, in the Gharbiyya governorate, where his father was a civil servant in the Waqf ministry. Afifi's parents were originally from Al-Zawaamil, another small town in the Sharqiyya governorate, but when they left Zifta, it was for Cairo, where they took up residence in Shubra. It is here that he met I'tidal Al-Saafi, a neighbor, whom he married in 1950. His father was eager for him to study law, the proper trajectory for the post of minister, and so the dutiful son graduated from Cairo University with a degree in law in 1943. However, Afifi could not repress his serious literary inclinations. Furthermore, he had already developed what was to be a lifelong abhorrence of authority and all its trappings. So, after finishing his degree, he decided to ignore parental expectations and changed fields, obtaining a second diploma from Cairo University's Institute of Journalism, the precursor of today's

Faculty of Media. In 1946 he published *Anwaar* (Lights), a novel and a collection of short stories, at his own expense. On the strength of *Anwaar,* he obtained an introduction to Mustafa and Ahmed Amin, founders of *Axbaar Al-Yawm,* a prominent daily newspaper, and was quickly hired. Except for a six year interval at rival *Dar Al-Hilaal* in the middle of his career, Afifi was employed there for the rest of his life. Over the course of the next thirty-odd years, his writings were also published in the magazines *Idhak* (Laugh), *Musaamaraat Al-Gayb* (Pocket entertainment), *Aaxir Saa'a* (The latest), and *Al-Kawaakib* (The stars). Afifi was the author of the popular columns "For Adults Only"; "Smile, Please"; and "Between You and Me," the first two of which have been collected and published in book form. He also wrote the scenarios for several films made in the 1960s. However, his writings were not exclusively confined to the realms of comedy and fiction. He also published a series of articles, *Sikkat Safar* (The journey), in book form, on the 1967 Arab-Israeli war.

Afifi was an eclectic and voracious reader. In fact, on his death, his rich collection was donated to the Egyptian national library. He also read French and English, and early in his career, he translated some short stories from world literature (Dostoevsky, Turgenev) into Arabic. A lifelong aficionado of all sorts of humor, it was in fact Afifi who, ubeknownst to many, translated the captions for the Mickey Mouse comic strip, famous in Egypt as Miiki. He was also eager to provide a venue for the creative output of his fellow countrymen, and to this end, he founded the well-known magazine *Al-Qissa* (The short story). It is thus no surprise that his journalistic writings continued to be interspersed by works of a more literary character. Besides *Anwaar,* Afifi has three novels to his credit: *Al-Tuffaaha wal-Gumguma* (1966, The apple and the skull), which was made into a radio play and a film, *Hikaayat Bint Ismaha Marmar* (1967, The story of a girl named Marmar), and *Fantaazia Fir'uuniyya* (1973, Pharaonic fantasy). He is also the author of *Taa'ih Fii London* (Lost in London), published after a stay there in 1968, *Daahikaat Saarixa* (Screaming laughs), *Al-Qitta wal-Sihliyya* (The cat and the salamander), and his last work, a fictionalized memoir, *Taraniim Fii Dhill Tamaara* (1984, *Little Songs in the Shade of Tamaara*). In 1978, President Sadat conferred upon him the prestigious national prize for artistic creativity. Diagnosed with throat cancer in the late 1970's, Mohammed Afifi died in 1981. He is survived by his wife, their three sons, and several grandchildren, all of whom still live in Cairo.

৯৫

In his all-too-short fictionalized memoir, Mohammed Afifi introduces himself to the reader as an old man, a man with arthritic fingers and knees. Precariously perched on an old straw chair under a tree in his garden, he reflects on the meaning of life. Afifi was only in his late fifties as he wrote, but he was gravely ill and died just after completing this little gem. However, his self-deprecating portrait cannot disguise the fact that his mind was as limber and graceful as the branches under which he sat and observed the goings-on in his beloved garden. Still, *Taraniim* is ineffably sad. This is a farewell portrait. Neither Afifi nor his garden would survive for long. The trials of contemporary Egypt—war, poverty, emigration, and the specter of an insatiable urbanization—have not stopped at his gate. The modern world is clearly none too benign, and the reader cannot help but wonder just how precarious Egypt's perch in it is. Yet despite this ominous undertone, here is a man whose heart is full of wonder and curiosity, whose eyes, ears, and nose are wide open to the delights of the natural world, and whose wit is sharp and acerbic, capable of exposing the sublime and the ridiculous in the society that revolves around his garden home.

Taraniim takes the reader through the cycle of seasons in an Egyptian garden, where Afifi spends as much of every day as possible. The garden is his paradise, whose inhabitants, whether animal or vegetable, he affectionately names and with whom he secretly converses. Queen of the realm is Tamaara, the *tamarhinna* tree in whose shade he muses by day, and in whose heavenly perfume he basks at sunset. Afifi, however, is as sensitive to the meek and lowly as he is to the majestic and beautiful. The mysterious world of frog and ant thus share the limelight with other more traditionally poetic creatures. In these lyrical meditations, Afifi reveals himself to his reader with surprising candor. He makes no effort to mask his childlike affection for the garden and its denizens, yet he is anything but sentimental. Afifi regales the reader with captivating scenes, at times endearing, at times horrific. He has the acute eye of a naturalist, and a delicious combination of reverence for the natural world and irreverence for social convention. One cannot fail to recognize the surreptitious pleasure Afifi derives from the company of Fido, the gardener's mangy dog, despite his wife's righteous objections to such an unclean guest. His eagerness to disabuse the love of his life of her devout notions of the praying mantis is equally clear. The insect's Arabic name, the Prophet's Horse, cloaks it in a pious aura that belies the ferocity of the female of the species, and Afifi, with cool detachment, depicts the gruesome mating ritual for his wife blow-by-blow.

Echoes of the wider world also reverberate within the sanctum of the garden: nightmarish echoes of a son reduced to cinders in the war, lighthearted echoes of another son's exotic snowy winter in unpronounceable Massachusetts, foreboding echoes of relentless urban expansion. From start to finish, *Taraniim* is laced with an undercurrent of irony. A master of dialogue as well, Afifi's conversations with his wife and Gum'a, the gardener, furnish the reader with an unforgettable gallery of characters. His garden is both a microcosm of the greater world and a window onto it. Here are good and evil, innocence and pomposity, humor and stodginess, instinct and calculation, selflessness and greed, ambition and contentment.

The brilliance of *Taraniim* lies perhaps in the fact that such an unusually intimate portrait is nevertheless so universal. In the gentle shade of Mohammed Afifi's prose, the reader discovers a wonderfully unassuming, lovingly ironic, deeply authentic Egyptian voice.

Preface

This is the last thing that Mohammed Afifi wrote before moving on to the next world. No doubt, Mohammed Afifi's next world will be of the simplicity, beauty, clarity, and honesty that marked his first life, his earthly life . . . the house and garden in which he lived his life, especially his last days, contemplating what surrounded him with the eye of an artist and poet and philosopher.

What is most beautiful in this book is the denial of the artistic self—if such an expression is possible. Afifi writes of the world around him, the world in which he finds himself and of which he is even the axis. Still, you do not feel for a moment that he, the author, is there. He transforms himself into a frame or a magical moving lens. This he aims at various details and aspects of daily life in such a way that, through it, you see the ordinary transformed into something extraordinary, into a work of art. Everything I have seen through Mohammed Afifi's magical lens, absolutely everything, acquires a strange translucence. This translucence speaks to you: things divulge their intrinsic essence, their secrets, their beautiful secrets. Or the secrets of their beauty. All things, even the simplest—a patch of light on the garden chairs, jasmine flowers on a carpet, peoples' faces in the pansies, cats, dogs, insects, birds, life, illness, death—are transformed into crystal clear images, around which a white butterfly flutters, grazing them with the delicate wings of Mohammed Afifi's style. This style floats with ease and consummate grace between, on the one hand, science and scientific analysis of life's observable phenomena, and on the other, ironic philosophical and artistic reflection on that life.

Were these lines Mohammed Afifi's last prayers? Were they the prayers and praise of an artist approaching his maker through artistic contemplation of the wonders of what He, the Almighty Artist, had created?

Hilmi Al-Touni

On the Old Yellow Straw Chair

Observations in a sunny garden on types of animals and birds and trees and a few human beings by an old man who sits on the aforementioned chair.

❧

MOHAMMED AFIFI

Chapter One

A new butterfly every day—a lemon on the
black cat's head—the sauce and its meaning—
what birds say—the perplexed frog—
tea the flavor of morning light

The White Butterfly

The white butterfly flashes on top of the high hedge fence as is her habit every morning, and, as is mine, I regret having to discount the lovely feeling that she is the same butterfly who visits my garden every day. But no one can expropriate my freedom to suppose what I will, and in my heart I have named that one hypothetical butterfly Faroosha, Flutterby. Faroosha flutters here and there, in search of her sustenance, until a banquet of colors in the pansy bed attracts her. She dives into it, landing on one of the flowers with outstretched wings to drink lovingly from the sweet nectar. Beside her is a flower on which is traced, in yellow and brown, the face of a small laughing monkey and another of a frightened purple child. A lovely place for a lovely white butterfly.

Next to me where I have seated myself on the old yellow straw chair, taking shade from my dear friend Tamaara, dozens of little white circles of light fall through her branches. They settle about me like dancing silver pennies on the green grass that covers the ground around me and on the round table of rough white pine—dark white, if you can say that. On top of the table rests the big brown china teacup whose handle broke long ago, for deliverance from which I thanked God. A penny has fallen on the surface of the tea, playfully, like a winking eye. It will be lovely to taste tea the flavor of morning light.

Here I love to sit in this mild weather at the beginning of fall, when I enjoy the warmth of the sun without its sting. It's not for Tamaara's smell that I sit beneath her. She rarely perfumes the air—only just before sundown as day turns over its keys to night. Amina was amazed the first time I told her years ago that I had named this tree Tamaara, but it wasn't long before she admitted:

—Well, by the Prophet, it suits her.

So I said, explaining the secret behind the name:

—— What would I call a *tamarhinna* tree anyway except Tamaara?

—— Well, do you have to call it by name?

—— Of course, so she knows I'm talking to her.

Amina knew I liked to talk to trees (answers not expected, of course), and she contented herself, by way of commentary, with a sarcastic cluck and a joking:

—— May God endow you with a brain.

As for Zahiira, she knows how she got her name. At first, Benzahiira, after her type of lemons. Then, day by day, the "b" dissolved in all those cups of juice until she became Zahiira.

Zahiira's branches touch those of her neighbor Tamaara, and here and there they interlace in a clear demonstration of love and affection. Naturally, Zahiira looks proud of all the ripe yellow fruits with which she is laden, fruits bursting with juice just the way Benzahiir should. A wise man of old once visited Egypt, and seeing them, he said, "I was amazed at how these people could get sick when they have lemons." There's no doubt his hunch was right about the benefits of lemons, long before people knew anything about vitamins. To discover their value, he probably didn't need to do much more than lift a yellow one like this to his nose and smell it. Or perhaps he scratched one with his fingernail and rubbed his beard with the healing juice that beaded up on its peel. He must have filled himself a cup every day and drunk it first thing each morning so that he might grow wiser.

Two birds have landed on Zahiira. They screech at one other, and then go on to argue about some common concern. A long time ago, I used to think birds were courting, and as the poet said, exchanging secrets in the sweetest of melodies. But long sittings in the garden have taught me otherwise. More often than not, the truth of the matter is that they are fighting, exchanging the foulest curses they know. I try to imagine the sort of curses birds would exchange, but fail, my mind only filling with human obscenities of which I am quick to clear this lovely species of winged creature.

The birds soon fly off, after giving the branch a good shake, dislodging a big yellow lemon, which falls onto the head of the black and white cat. This may be why I'd rather sit under Tamaara than Zahiira; I doubt I'd be happy with a big lemon in the brown china cup of tea. Before this, the cat had been asleep on the green grass. Like me, she'd been enjoying the warmth of the dancing white pennies. Now she becomes aware of the sound of the birds, lifts her head, and trains on them two sleepy green eyes. As always happens in circumstances like these, her lips and her whiskers twitch with a quivering, muted meow, the bitter embodiment of her desperate longing for that flying protein. Looking at those trembling jaws, I can almost hear her say:

— Lord! You created birds for us to eat and to sing your praises for, but why, oh Lord, why did you create wings for them to escape us with??

And it is at this moment that the yellow lemon falls on her black head, a punishment, perhaps, for her objection to the creator's will. She leaps up in terror, turning this way and that in an attempt to discover the secret of what has happened. For a moment she fixes me—the only person around—with a green gaze of accusation. But soon she forgets the whole business, and stretches her cavernous jaws in a yawn. In the beginning, of course, her name was Buusi,* like all middle-class Egyptian cats. However, her owner,

---

*For Pussy. Arabic has no "p" and so foreign loan words containing one usually turn up with a "b" instead.

Hamada, suddenly began to call her Muuni, and with every passing day, she became more responsive to this new name. When asked the reason for the change, he answered with the lisp that stuck with him until he was over five:

— Thee told me that wath her name.

But of course it all boiled down to his having chosen a name with no "s" that he could pronounce more easily.

Muuni lifts her head to sniff the air. As usual, she is quicker than I to catch the appetizing smell that has begun to perfume the air of the garden. Now *ta'liya* comes with *muluxiyya,** and it is rare for *muluxiyya* to appear without chicken, or rabbit, at the very least. This is a chain of deductions I do not claim passed so clearly through that black brain, though I wouldn't entirely rule it out in a cat of twenty, by our counting—over a hundred in cat years, that is.

The smell wafts from the open balcony door, having passed through the living room by way of the small corridor that leads to the kitchen. There I imagine Amina, in her gray dress, standing in the midst of a

---

*Ta'liya is an aromatic garlic and coriander sauce, the necessary final touch to the famous Egyptian green soup, *muluxiyya.*

thick white cloud of steam issuing from the pots. In the face of that smell, Muuni forgets all about the sun and bounds off toward the balcony with surprising alacrity.

Then comes a rustle from under the hedge. I know its source before I look, before I face the bulging black eyes of the creature who stands staring at me questioningly. It is the big frog—or frogess—who appears from time to time and whom I have allowed myself to presume—unlike the white butterfly—to be one and the same frog.

— Aawww!

It's one concise word he says to me each time he passes by. Then he makes a leap that takes him through the hedge to the shed yard behind it. Froggie, I've named him, presuming he's a male. If he's a she, she'll just have to add a feminine *-ess*.

A small white body darts out of the pansy bed, the butterfly who's had her fill of nectar and flown. For a long time I've wondered if a butterfly gets full so quickly because its stomach is small or because—due to a certain cunning in her nature—she refuses to take a complete meal from one flower, preferring to fill her stomach from twenty flowers in twenty gardens.

At that, I remember my cup of tea and reach

toward it a hand whose bulbous veins I've grown accustomed to seeing, trying to ignore the slight tremor that lately has disfigured it. This is why I welcomed the loss of the china teacup's handle. Now I hold it in both hands instead of with two or three fingers, which used to make the tremor more obvious. But the tea is truly delicious, with that added flavor of morning light, and I take my time sipping it on the yellow straw chair.

Chapter Two

Does Gum'a require veiling?—a migrating bird
in the kitchens of London—a rusty water wheel
named Shahata—Fido or His Master's Voice,
the impure, banished dog

Amina and Hamada and Fido

The dancing pennies of light beneath Tamaara still give me enough warmth here where I sit on the old yellow straw chair. In front of me, under Zahiira, there is another green chair from the same old set. It is Amina's favorite when she comes down to the garden, because, as she says, green is the color of paradise.

Out of the house and onto the porch comes Amina, in her gray dress, a long *sibha** with little black beads hanging from her hand. She's not satisfied with a *sibha* of fewer than a hundred beads: the thirty-bead

---

*The *sibha* is a very popularly used string of beads, similar to a rosary, that helps the devotee count prayers. There are strings of different lengths, and beads of many different types.

variety she leaves for amateurs whose faith has yet to reach its fullness.

Before, she would wear nothing but black. Over time, though, I convinced her that gray was just as eloquent an expression of sadness, and an even more dignified one. On her head is a white scarf to hide her hair from men's eyes, although her hair is practically whiter than the scarf. One day I said to her mockingly:

— Are there any men in the garden, Amina?

She replied angrily:

— Isn't Gum'a a man?

And I thought of replying:

— Well, if you're a woman, he's a man.

But of course I didn't. Not everything a person thinks should be said, especially if it's true.

Heavily, Amina walks along the balcony, swaying from side to side to distribute the pains of her rheumatism evenly on each leg. She comes down the four steps that lead to the garden and crosses the little sand pathway, killing, for sure, a fair number of the ants in the column that is always at work there.

Amina has gotten heavier and heavier. In fact, she's almost fat. Graceful dark gazelle with the hazel eyes . . . Delightful traces of an elusive green danced in their depths. The beautiful Amuuna, my Amuuna . . . How many nicknames I pampered her with in the early days of our marriage.

She eases her body onto the green straw chair, and says:

— The rheumatism's really giving me what for today.

A certain roughness has crept into her voice since she hit sixty, and she doesn't try to hide it. She lets her thoughts wander for a bit, and then opens her favorite topic of conversation:

— Hamada's late with his letter this time.

— Do you think people in America have time for letters?

— He could just send me a couple of lines so I wouldn't worry. What did you say the name of that place he's in is?

She can't pronounce Massachusetts to save her life.

— The devil take them, them and their names! What kind of a name is that to call a place? Well, it serves him right! Here he was at home with us, in the lap of luxury, waited on hand and foot, and he has to go traipsing off to the ends of the earth? And I wish I could say it was for something worthwhile! But no, even now it's only the grace of God that's keeping him going.

— Just give him a little time. He'll find his footing soon enough.

It was natural that she should become doubly attached to Hamada after what happened. To keep him from emigrating she used every tactic, including illness. But she was wasting her breath: the boy decided to fly the coop, and that was that. Before he skipped west over the Atlantic, he wrote to us from London saying he was earning his living washing dishes in restaurants. Amina almost fell over.

— Oh no! My Hamada washing dishes? He never even once put his hand in the sink. Why, when he'd make coffee, I'd wash the *kanaka* for him!

I reassure her that in those countries they use a machine to wash dishes, not human hands, and that she doesn't need to imagine her son holding a British dishrag to scrub dirty dishes still soiled with pork grease. This soothes her somewhat, though the very idea of washing dishes remains a terrible insult. How could her son, a respectable young man with a cum laude B.A. in business, accept it?

A hoarse voice calls us from behind the hedge, the voice of Gum'a, the shed guard, who is responsible for watering and raking the garden.

— Good morning, Bey, good morning, Hagga, I've got some beautiful arugula today!

— Bring us two bunches.

— Of course, Hagga.

— And radishes, too.

— Of course, Bey.

— And a few of your eggs, too.

As if the designated hen has heard us, she begins clucking the way a hen does when she's going to lay. Meanwhile, from the back of the shed, that endless faint moan reaches us. It is the crying of Shahata, Gum'a's son, a sound more like the creaking of a rusty old water wheel than anything else.

Amina gets up and disappears around the back of the house. After a while, Gum'a appears at the low, iron garden gate, his flabby body lost in his flowing white *galabiyya* that's big enough for two more like him. A thick black mustache presides over his dark round face. It looked scary at first. Later it reminded me more of the ones actors put on for comic roles. At Gum'a's side is his laughable dog with the dark brown hairless back and the dark yellow belly. In spite of this, he has auspiciously named him Fido, like the dogs of the well-to-do.

Gum'a pushes the gate open, and Fido starts to follow, but he stops him.

— Back, Fido, back; don't get the Hagga mad at us.

The dog is not allowed in the garden on Amina's orders. Not because he's been bad in any way, but just because he is a dog. This charge makes of him—and all the dogs of the world—an impure creature we must spurn, avoid, and scold whenever we see him.

Once I thought to ask her:

— So why did the Lord create him?

She answered firmly:

—Why did he create the scorpion?

I didn't argue with her, and so we were deprived of a dog of our own that might guard us from misguided thieves. The dog barks in protest at having been stopped from coming in, and in his voice there is the same hoarseness as in Gum'a's. Was it strange, then, that I name him His Master's Voice? But he stays outside despite the open gate, throwing himself onto the sidewalk and lifting a leg to bite his yellow belly, hunting for any ticks he might find there. A practical cross between cleaning and nutrition.

I like Gum'a for some reason I don't completely understand, and at the same time I pity him. It amazes me that he takes himself seriously, working so he can marry and start a family, sitting up at night to smoke his water pipe and set about having another child. But then there are a lot of things I have learned to love and pity from where I sit here on the old yellow straw chair.

Chapter Three

Green that isn't green—a league of birds and
Gum'a's family—a scratched record that
moans—why does Gum'a use the masculine
pronoun when talking about the wounded duck?

Rina and the Palm Tree and the Male Duck

Even Tamaara's warm pennies aren't welcome on this almost summery morning. Winter continues to drag its feet for some unclear reason; no doubt it's cooking up something special for us in its unhallowed kitchen. So I sit on the porch on the red straw chair, the third of the old set. This, after having gathered up all the jasmine blossoms that, as usual, cover it.

God bless you wherever you are, Hamada! It is Hamada who brought a few jasmine branches inside, and with some string and nails, made for us on the balcony a charming little thicket of jasmine. Mother

Jasmine continues her slow, tireless journey toward the roof of the house. Dozens of white blossoms gleam against her green, giving me what I tend to think are sympathetic looks.

Here on the porch I can see almost all of my fourth friend from behind the hedge, which only blocks the lower part of her long trunk. She is my friend without being my tree. But since when has ownership been among the conditions of friendship? She grows in the shed yard, on what we jokingly call Uncle Gum'a's land, since he is in charge of watching over the bags of cement and iron bars kept there that belong to the contractor who owns the land.

Ever tall and graceful and harmonious, green without being green. A touch of reddish brown mixes with her soft green to make her no single precise color. Sometimes she's an orangey green, sometimes yellow, and sometimes an incandescent brick, practically red. In her love of uniqueness, she has refused to have leaves like any other trees, depending for her breathing on those little twigs that dangle from her branches the way fringes dangle from the sleeve of a green dress on a graceful girl like herself.

But Amina doesn't like her and doesn't deny it.

— I can't understand what you see in her. No fruit, no blossoms, no use whatsoever.

In her relationship with plants, she's of the usefulness school. This is why she likes the palm tree at the back of the shed yard. It's a glum tree, leaning at an acute angle that makes its life a constant struggle against falling. But it still bears fruit and feeds Gum'a and his family from the lone, red bunch of dates it produces each summer. That's in addition to its numerous historical connections to prophets and saints.

Pointing to my friend, I say to Amina:

—You know what this one's name is?

Making a show of patience, she says:

—What, pray tell?

— Her name is Rina.

Mockingly, she asks:

— How come?

— Now what would I call a casuarina tree but Rina??

Amina laughs a little laugh, though she used to laugh a lot before what happened, and then she says:

— May God endow you with a brain.

In the back of the shed yard, near the palm tree, is that yellow stone building. Birds have turned the dozens of fissures in its walls into as many nests. Back there is where they store sacks of cement and iron spikes and Uncle Gum'a's family, and from there issues that rusty moan that stops neither day nor night.

Of Shahata's mother I know nothing but her primitive rude voice that resounds in the shed yard whenever she and her husband Gum'a fight. Luckily for me, I can't understand anything she says, as the words pour out of her mouth in a single burst, the way gravel pours out of the back of a dump truck.

In the beginning he used to cry the way all children cry, fits of screaming that subside when the cause for them does. But then it became apparent that the cause never did subside for Shahata. With effort and exertion, the crying turned into a soft, continuous moan, like the scratch of a broken record eternally stuck on the word "Aah." Maybe it was hunger at that emaciated woman's breast, or maybe it was colic or diarrhea or mosquito repellent. But it was a sound I got used to and that ceased to bother me. Maybe I'd even have missed it and been bothered by its absence had it stopped.

——Why don't you take him to a doctor, Gum'a?

That's what I suggested one day. He answered:

— Just one doctor, Bey? I've been to every hospital in town. Bless the Prophet,* Bey.

He pointed at the stone house and said:

— It's all that woman's fault! May it never befall you and yours . . . Her insides are no good . . . She's never once had a healthy baby.

Amina found out from the milkman that two of Gum'a's children had already died. That was why this last one had been named Shahata, to deflect the eyes of the envious from him, so that he might live.†

---

*This set phrase is used in a variety of contexts. Here, among other things, it emphasizes Gum'a's seriousness, and injects a note of piety into the discussion. Furthermore, because a set reply can be expected (though none is offered here), it is a discourse strategy that seeks to draw the listener even more actively into the conversation.

†A frightening potency is attributed to envy. At its worst, envy is deemed capable of destroying its object. An envious glance may be enough to do damage. Hence the concept of the evil eye. Naturally, people are particularly leery of envy's pernicious effects on what they prize most highly. Thus, infants and young children are feared to be at great risk. However, the eye is not envy's only vehicle. Lavish praise may also denote suspect emotions. Talismans of one sort or another are popular safeguards against envy. Naming, in this case, is purely talismanic. Shahata means beggary. It is hoped that no one will envy the bearer of such an inauspicious name.

— Missus! Mudam!* Hagga!

It's Gum'a's voice at the garden gate, which I can't see from here. Amina's voice answers from the kitchen.

— Come in, Gum'a. Do you want something?

I don't hear what he answers, as his dog decides to bark with him at the same instant.

Amina says:

— Let me see it.

Says Gum'a:

— Beat it, Fido! Beat it!

The sound of an argument between them, which I can't make anything out of, comes from the door of the kitchen. Gum'a's hoarse voice tries to rise, but Amina's gets the upper hand and brings him up short. Then they both stop, and a minute passes before that strange creature appears before me on the sand pathway.

It is an ordinary black duck like all ducks, no doubt, but right away I'm sure there's something unnatural about her. It takes me a few moments to discover that something: the long trickle of bright red

---

*Gum'a's inaccurate pronunciation of this foreign word which has made its way into mainstream Egyptian colloquial locates him squarely—and humorously—among the illiterate.

blood dripping from the duck's neck and drawing on the sand below it a long, weaving red line. She can't be a duck with a hemorrhage. She's so weak that she takes two steps and falls. Rising again with great effort, she doesn't realize that she is taking her last steps. Then she sees something attractive on the ground, pecks at it, and raises it up to swallow it, all awash in her own blood.

Gum'a appears then, coming down the path. No sooner does he see the duck than he shouts happily:

— I found him, Missus.

I am surprised to hear him refer to the duck as a he until he says:

—That's a male duck your wife's been asking me to get for her.

He swoops down on the bird and grabs him, holding him by the legs, head dangling. The trickle of blood has by now turned into a gushing stream.

Seeking an explanation, I ask:

— She's been slaughtered?

He corrects me:

—Yes, he has.

— Are you the one who slaughtered him?

— Of course, Bey.

—Well, couldn't you do it right? He's run around the whole garden.

He replies proudly:

— It's better that way, sir. Gets rid of all his blood.

Then, moving off with the victim, he says:

—Your very good health, Bey!

With all my heart, I long to take off my shoe, head after him, and give him a drubbing,* but of course it remains just a wish. After all, where is the sin in what Gum'a has done? Has he desecrated holy writ?†

As for me, I don't think I will put a single piece of that poor male into my mouth. Not unless, God forbid, a regrettable episode of forgetfulness should overcome me . . . but how often such episodes overcome me lately.

---

*A beating with a shoe is especially demeaning because of the additional indignity of a shoe's impurity.

†Traditional societies value the tried and true, and are wary of innovation. In the realm of religious law, which regulates slaughter, innovation is out of the question. Afifi, the animal lover, incorporates a humorously discordant archaic expression here that has the effect of emphasizing what a reluctant observer he is to this, traditionally speaking, rather unremarkable slaughter.

Amina comes onto the porch, drying her hands on a towel, and says triumphantly:

— A male duck worth two pounds, and I got it from him for just one!

I think about it for a minute and say:

— It's better that way. Gets rid of all his blood!

Not understanding, Amina says:

—What's that supposed to mean?

Tersely, I say:

— A bad joke.

Chapter Four

*Does sadness clash with flowers?—a special
kind of love—a scandal among gardens—
I'm no better than the white butterfly—
the happiness of the lost boy*

*A Scandal in the World
of Gardens*

— Why don't you plant the garden, Bey, rather
than leaving it bare like this?

That is what Gum'a said to me one day when he
had just started working in our garden. At the time, I
answered him evasively:

— It is planted, just look.

— These are trees, sir. I mean plant it with roses
and flowers and cheerful stuff like that that'll make it
smile and look pretty.

It hadn't occurred to him that that was the very
secret behind this mournful garden, that Amina didn't

want it to laugh or be pretty. How could she, after what had happened?

I asked Gum'a jokingly:

— Why don't you plant those flowers at your place?

— Are we the type for flowers, Bey? It's enough that we have radishes and arugula. Shall I get out the hoe and come tomorrow?

— No, Gum'a, give it time.

I risked laying out the idea for Amina during one of her calm moments, emphasizing to her the fact that this insistence on sadness and forbidding the small joys of life that God has permitted was nothing but a hidden refusal of God's will and a silent objection to it.

— At least submit the subject to the office of the mufti.

God bless Mufida, the sheikha* who leads the weekly religion class that Amina has attended for years. She's an open-minded sheikha with broad horizons, who was in complete agreement with me about

---

*The feminine form of sheikh, literally an elder. Here, it designates a woman with particular knowledge of religious doctrine and practice. Informal religious study groups are becoming increasingly popular in Egypt.

Amina's eternal sadness, although she had opposed me earlier about the dog, His Master's Voice, sentencing him to everlasting impurity.

Gum'a's smile reached his ears when I gave him permission to plant the garden, stipulating that he do so within very strict limits. It was delightful to watch Gum'a at work in the garden. He would break up the earth with the hoe, exposing its black insides, thirsty for light, to the sun. Or with the spade he would caress it gently, as if afraid he might injure it. His hand would sink into the moist black soil, as if sinking into dough that had been moistened with milk and honey.

He loves the earth with the heart of a true farmer whom cruel fortune has reduced to the station of a guard of cement sacks. I myself could walk on the earth for a whole lifetime without loving it like that. I might build a castle or a pyramid on it, or dig myself a grave in it, but none of that would make me love it with this kind of love.

It is, of course, a blatant scandal in the world of gardening, this garden that Gum'a has planted. A scandal, at least, by the standards of those who use words like tulip and gladiolus and who plant other such flowers of noble descent. A pansy bed of a hundred colors, where the impudent monkey stands next to the frightened rabbit, next to the girl who's just stepped out of the hairdresser's. And other new shapes are there to be discovered every day, if one is so inclined. Another bed, with a variety of brilliant shades of red, reminds me of nothing so much as the dresses girls wear on an outing at the zoo on the first morning of the *eid*.*

However, this does not bother me. How could it bother a man who considers himself a fanatic supporter of botanic socialism? All flowers are beautiful in my view, as long as they bring me joy. As for noble origins, let's leave them for those who need them. How could I not love that monkey and that rabbit, that yellow Chinese man with the long black mustache whose presence I just discovered the other day? The little white butterfly loves these flowers and rushes to them. Who am I to pretend that I know more about flowers than the little white butterfly?

Pointing proudly to his handiwork, Gum'a says to me:

— See, Bey? Honestly . . . isn't it a beaut?
— By the sweat of your brow, Gum'a!

---

*Feast or holiday. This is the word used for all of the major religious holidays, whether Christian or Muslim.

— How about if I plant you a bed that goes clear around?

— Ask the missus.

A few days later, I see him busy turning over the earth around the periphery of the grass. And Amina, not looking at me, says:

— I'll tell you something if you won't laugh.

— Why should I laugh?

— You know how you are.

— I won't laugh.

Embarrassed, she says:

— Mohammed* came to me in a dream and told me he was happy that we planted the garden.

I reach out my hand to stroke her old knee tenderly, here where she sits before me on the old green straw chair the color of paradise.

And I say to her sincerely:

— May God always make both of you happy.

I press her knee gently, and, in pain but with a vestige of her former coquettishness, she says:

— Ayyy, the rheumatism!

---

*Hamada is a nickname for the given name Mohammed. The use of the formal name is another clue to the seriousness with which Amina regards her dream.

Chapter Five

The Scandal of the Hoopoe

If winter comes, then spring can't be far behind
. . . nonsense some cold English poet wrote to steel
himself to his misfortune. He of all people should
know that when winter comes, it comes and that
between him and spring there are long months of cold
distress and icy misery.

How glad I am then to see it delay its arrival like
this. In a moment of madness I even imagine that it
might have canceled its coming altogether, moved by
an ardent prayer from my pure heart! But winter is
winter, a cold word we must hear from Time whenever the ordained moment arrives.

And so, one morning I open the balcony door, and

it is as if I'd opened the door of a great, universal freezer that threatens to solidify anything it touches. I close it in a hurry and wave to my friends from behind the glass. Not one of them returns my greeting. Mournful, all of them, pale, carrying the weight of the whole world. Glancing up at the sky, I see why: a dismal, gray sky threatening a nasty winter's day. Nevertheless, the air is absolutely still. Not a single leaf on a single branch of the thousands of motionless branches around me stirs, a disquieting frozen calm, like the moments of a countdown before the explosion of the calamity the sky has prepared for us.

Stupidly, Muuny lies down in front of the heater, amazed not to feel its expected warmth, imagining that if she stares at it long enough she might turn it on with the power of her hidden magic. She is the goddess Basiit, the spirit of Isis, mistress of magic. She does not know that gas has become a precious fuel, and that wise people no longer turn on heaters in the morning. And, of course, it means nothing to her at all, that word OPEC.

Amina is the real winner today, standing in front of the hot burners of the stove with the rattling pots that fill the air with a warm, appetizing steam. I have only to listen from afar to that melodious sound to be filled with warmth, the sound of the ladle as it is banged against the sides of a hot pot.

I stand behind the closed glass, rubbing my palms together and blowing on them, cursing winter and all its forefathers. Suddenly, something lands on the balcony wall, something alive, embroidered with shades of brown and dark beige. On his head, a proud red crown, and in front of him, in the guise of a bill, a long sharp sword. A beautiful hoopoe . . . I'd been taught from my childhood to love this bird and to take him as a good omen and to wish for some of the blessings that scatter from his wings when he flies.

I am delighted with him for having chosen my balcony to honor with his landing, and I rebuke him when he quickly spreads his wings and flies off over the hedge. Crossing the whole shed yard until he reaches the stone house with the fissures, he alights on its roof, above Gum'a and his family and the sparrows.

For a moment, I turn my attention from him to watch the sky, which has begun to take on an ugly black. I am brought back to him by the noise that suddenly issues from his direction, where a big whirlwind of birds wheels above the stone house in feverish circles, all screeching at once. In the midst of that whirlwind I see an embroidered body, the hoopoe. He has moved from the roof of the house to its fissured walls, where he is holding on with his claws, beating his wings rapidly to keep from falling. His long sharp bill has penetrated into the depths of one of the fissures, ransacking it with a clear, unmistakable purpose, the utter destruction of that nest.

Why he has chosen this particular one I don't know, and why Hoopoe and Sparrow should be enemies I don't know. There is nothing I can do but stand here helplessly, watching that tragic sight. Many things the hoopoe pulls out of the nest, scattering them about him in the air. I make out feathers, leaves, twigs. In my fevered imagination, I see a batch of eggs that has not hatched yet, or a family of baby birds with outstretched necks and open bills waiting for what their mother will stuff into them on her return.

It is clear from the hoopoe's enthusiasm that he is taking great pleasure in his work, a pleasure inscrutable to all but his kind. As for me, I will remain eternally ignorant of whether this hoopoe has decided—on a sudden human impulse—to destroy that nest just for the joy of destruction, or if he is having his usual breakfast as he does every day, unbeknownst to me.

The hoopoe finally tires or feels full or gets bored or whatever, and gives a flap of his wings that lifts him up onto the roof of the stone house. He stands there turning about conceitedly, his crown dancing above his head with the vanity of the triumphant, his sword stretched out before him as if to say, "Any challengers?" The birds are still wheeling madly about him, afraid the brute might just be resting before swooping down on a new nest.

Suddenly there is a crash of thunder, then a second and a third. A sword lights up the sky, piercing the thick black clouds, and the sky opens up with the anticipated cosmic shower that inundates everything —Rina and Zahiira and Tamaara and the old yellow straw chair, and the other green one, the color of paradise, and the laughing monkeys and the frightened children and the girls' red and pink dresses. The white butterfly, thank God, is too smart to come out in such weather.

The hoopoe, terrified, flies from the stone roof, somewhat damp blessings scattering from his wings. The sparrows return to their nests hurriedly, and I feel sorry that they have no doors behind which to shelter from the evils of life.

If only the sky had been a bit quicker with the rain it might have saved that poor nest from destruction.

But then again, who knows? Isn't it possible that this was the nest of a lax and dissolute sparrow who deserved the punishment meted out to him, that he might be an admonition to all birds who can heed a warning?*

Too late, I realize I should have called Amina to witness the scandal of that murderous hoopoe. I know that she will not believe me when I tell her the story. She will say that this blessed bird, a friend of the prophet Solomon, could not possibly commit a crime like this and that I have begun to imagine things that have no basis in fact because of my long association with trees and animals, sitting on the old yellow chair.

A stream of rain begins to beat against the glass, almost obscuring the view completely. I hate the whole scene and move away toward the heater, where Muuny is still waiting patiently. Yes, the wise no longer turn on heaters in the morning, but is there some blockhead out there who wants to relegate me, like it or lump it, to the camp of the wise?

---

*A tongue-in-cheek reference to Quranic stories of disaster that befall the wicked. A serious naturalist and a great believer in observation and scientific method, Afifi couldn't resist this dig at divine interpretations of tragedy.

Chapter Six

On the old, wine-colored carpet—snow
closed the doors—he came from the far ends of
Sinai—the boy and the black lump of coal—
love in the midst of the storm

Next to the Heater

The storm grumbles in the frozen darkness, angry and noisy in the midst of the meek, silent green things. The howl of the wind doesn't stop, nor does the painful groan of the soft parts of the tree trunks. On a night like this, any tree, even the tall, graceful one which I suspect is harmonious even now, may break and fall without anyone noticing. The cosmic shower has been running for hours, as if someone had turned it on to take a bath and forgotten to shut it off.

I sit down in the living room on the right of the lighted heater, in the robin's egg armchair that once was blue, with my feet on what is left of the plush of the old wine-colored carpet. Amina is on another chair like it, on the left of the heater. Her fingers, interlaced, search for warmth in front of its vents, hot with the promise of relief for our frozen old digits. Were we to claim that, once upon a time, we had extracted our own warmth from the depths of these two bodies, we might well be called liars.

Suddenly, a black on white body jumps into my lap. It is Muuny, who's been asleep and dreaming at my feet. My lap is better, being nearer the hot vents of the heater, and the gray wool robe radiates extra heat underneath her, so she rolls herself into a ball and begins to recite:

— Krrrrrr.

Inscrutable recitations that Amina insists are of a religious nature, nothing to be surprised at from a former goddess. I put my hand on her back, smoothing its black velvet, and extend a finger to feel the vibrations of her recitation beneath her white chin, which stretches in enjoyment.

— Krrrrrr!

Her voice rises, and Amina notices it and sighs.

— Oh, my dear, sweet boy! Here we are warm and comfy, and my own child can't even close the door for all the snow!

This is a piece of information Hamada has written to her in his last letter, one I am hard put to believe. Rolling up a ball of blue wool yarn, Amina continues:

— Well, I'll make him a nice pullover to keep him warm!

— You think there's a shortage of pullovers in America?

— A mother's handiwork keeps him warmer!

— Alas for orphans like us!

Suddenly the idea becomes clear in my mind and I say to her:

— Did you ever see a door that opened outwards?

And she says, not understanding:

— What do you mean?

— I mean when you go to open a door, do you pull it in or push it out?

She thinks a minute and says:

— I pull it in.

And I answer, in triumph, snapping my fingers:

— In America it must snow inside the houses!

But it seems she's thought the matter over on her own, because she replies very quickly:

— Their doors must be like that!

— They open outwards?

— Mm-hmm, whoever'd call a place Massakufitch would make the doors open outwards.

I love the false look of anger on her wheat-colored face that wrinkles have begun to invade. The old touch of green still plays in her eyes, though it has lost its brightness. But no one blames Amina or expects her to be her old self after what has happened. If they had told her that he had been martyred, it would have been easier for her than that cold, dry, terse word. Lost. They said it and stopped. Did their duty and left. No one explained to her how her eldest son had been transformed from present to lost. How he had strayed and how not a soul could point the way to him. They were long, grim weeks that Amina lived in the hospital, in a world not our own. Maybe she found her lost son there and was afraid to leave him, lest she lose him again. She lived in a world alone, week after week, in a world in whose cold twisted paths travelers most often lose their way forever. And then a man came running from the ends of the Sinai, undid the few remaining buttons of his khaki jacket, and threw himself down and said, panting for breath:

— Well, sir, half of us are lost. Can anybody tell one person from another? One of those bombs hits a truck with everybody in it and just turns them into a black lump of charcoal!

A lump of black charcoal, my son. It was an image

that horrified me for a long time, an image that almost broke me. Thank God it never reached Amina's ears in that other world of hers. Nevertheless, it was much easier for me to bear than the image of his body left out in the open, predators gnawing at his flesh in that holy land.

After a time, Amina came back to our world, but she was not—nor could she be—the same Amina who had left. Some of her stayed there and never came back, and some things came back but with a different color, like her hair which had been black and went white. Little by little she began to learn to smile again.

From above the blue ball of yarn, her voice reaches me:

— I don't know what would become of me if something happened to Hamada, too.

It is a remark I've heard from her more than once since Hamada emigrated, a remark she makes in the roughest of voices. Fortunately, I am never obliged to answer, because it is always directed at herself. She mulls it over deep down and doesn't wait to hear an answer. And if she ever does answer herself, I don't know what she says.

Contemplating her from above the knitting yarn

with love and pity, without her realizing it, I lean towards her and say:

— I love you, Amuuna.

She steals a surprised glance at me, smiles, and says:

— God love you!

Many a storm blew through our lives, and we weathered them, many a fire, and we extinguished them, and then what happened happened and it swept away everything in its path.

How it annoys me to hear the tree trunks' painful groan in the face of this crazy storm. Many lemons must have fallen from the branches of Zahiira before their time. Mud has covered the earth around the old yellow chair, and in it are little white leaves which have fallen from Tamaara, leaves that had been sweet-smelling.

— Krrrrrr!

Unconsciously, I take a handful of the hair on Muuny's back and rub it against its natural grain, a whim that often gets the better of a person when petting cats. Muuny growls (where she sleeps), announcing her anger, and even puffs up in a moment of ambiguity between dream and reality in her black skull.

Chapter Seven

The chair needs a nail—the sun came up on Isis—Muuny shares in building the pyramid—the goddess that fell—rescue at the last moment

---

Muuny

Prison in the house for two days. From behind the glass, I see Tamaara and Zahiira resist the storm with the same heroism. Beneath them, the lawn is covered with their fallen leaves that have turned the yellow straw chair to a green identical to its paradise-colored friend. I leave the balcony door and go collapse next to the heater on the robin's egg chair that used to be blue. The smell of the kitchen floods the living room, thick and concentrated. It's almost enough to make a person feel full. From time to time Amina comes in and sits down without talking to finish another line of the blue pullover, her ear pricked to the kitchen for the sound of a pot rattling, at which she puts down the yarn and hurries off.

Thank God that it is short-lived, this anger of the Egyptian winter at the sons of the Nile valley. Like the anger of a short-tempered father at his children, yelling and banging, shouting and throwing, a slap here and a punch there, and then suddenly it all blows over and clears up, and on the green earth the sun of peace shines once again.

And thus it is that, once again, I find myself free to roam the garden, wiping off the old yellow chair which the rains have washed and which has become even yellower. I pull it out from beneath Tamaara and put it smack in the sun, the holy, hot sun that will melt whatever has frozen the past two days in these dried-up old veins. Thanks go to Gum'a, who has swept the lawn of the withered, muddy leaves that covered it, and has sprinkled some sand around so that the ground will dry quickly.

This chair needs urgent repair, or I will regret it when its back leg breaks suddenly and I find myself lying next to it on the green grass that is still wet. I hope if I fall that Amina is not there, nor Gum'a, nor even Muuny. As for the trees, well, it's not a problem to fall in front of them because they don't laugh, or at least they know how to hide their laughter.

Muuny, too, is happy with the sun that has come out after an absence. She walks back and forth, here and there, with unusual sprightliness. She even flattens her belly to the ground once and jumps, clinging to Zahiira's trunk, escaping, just for fun, from a non-existent danger.

Muuny wanders over the lawn until she reaches a patch of ground whose grass has thinned. She sits down there and begins to look at me with interest, as if seeing me for the first time. On her rump she sits, gathering her tail around her, head up, green eyes considering me. Her front paws are planted before her like two columns of black granite at the door of an ancient temple. The only white is her chest and a part of her stomach, and it is as if the temple is lit from within. Dignified, serious, haughty, ready to receive the rituals due her whenever the worshipers choose.

The great Khufu himself almost went bankrupt at the hands of the tyrannical contractors who built his pyramid. The priests told him that no one would be able to rescue him from his predicament but the cat goddess, Basiit, worshipped in the eastern part of the Delta, near present day Zaqaziiq. So Khufu ordered that a big temple be built to her there and that the most delicious fat mice and birds be sacrificed to her in it. And since Khufu was delivered from the straits he was in and was able to finish building the pyramid, isn't it just possible that the crafty Basiit really is all-powerful?

She looks into my eyes piercingly, from the harsh depths of her green eyes. Evil is clear there; she can't hide it. Hateful, no doubt, towards the people of these times who have transformed her from a goddess to whom offerings are made to an animal to whom scraps are thrown. Her looks speak, and I can practically hear her saying:

— Listen, you! I don't mind keeping up appearances. What have we got to lose? But you know perfectly well that I despise you. Yes, I rub up against your leg from time to time, making a show of my love, and when I lie on your lap, I do a few recitations I know you like, but all these things are just the requirements of the job, nothing more. You and your tribe have inculcated in me fawning and dissembling, after you spent thousands of years fawning and dissembling before me. I am the goddess Basiit, the spirit of Isis, goddess of Magic, and I do not forget easily. One day, I will reclaim my lost glory, and then you will all know the meaning of the word vengeance!

With poisoned words like these she must have thrown terror into the sensitive hearts of my ancestors, and so they worshipped her to escape her wrath. Words that gush like volcanic lava from the depths of her wicked green eyes.

A strange cat has come creeping up behind her; it must be one of her grandchildren's grandchildren who are all over the neighborhood. He's a pale green, long-bodied cat, stretched like a sock that kids have stuffed with cotton. He approaches her little by little until his head is right at her backside; suddenly she senses his hot breath, and lightning quick, she turns and gives him a slap that would flatten a striped tiger or a spotted leopard. He runs off helter skelter, with no dignity, as sometimes happens among humans, in a fierce woman's moment of exceeding modesty in a crowded bus. Muuny moves off toward the balcony, the picture of displeasure, disgusted with this society that does not grant a virtuous woman a moment when she can sleep, secure in her honor.

Beneath the hedge, I hear a familiar rustle, and I look to see the protruding black eyes that belong to Froggie, who says to me inquiringly:

— Aawww!

I look around before I answer him, saying, out of courtesy, and in order not to embarrass him:

— Aawww!

He or she looks pleased and jumps a jump that takes him into the shed yard. I remember what I had read about frogs having become a great delicacy in the fancy restaurants of Europe, a specialty, in other words, of the elite. I had found out from someone who knew someone among that elite that its taste was a cross between fish and rabbit. This is hardly surprising in an amphibious creature who combines the characters of both water and land dwellers. But I got goose bumps imagining myself munching on the graceful thigh that jumps those lovely jumps and belongs to that sweet creature.

The holy hot sun bath has gotten even holier than is good for me, melting what had frozen in my veins and threatening to melt the veins themselves. I'd better move under the dancing pennies of my friend Tamaara. There beneath her I raise my arms and extend my legs to stretch. Suddenly I find myself tipping back, setting off on no uncertain journey towards the ground, seated as I am on the old yellow straw chair. Nothing saves me from this painful fate but Tamaara's trunk, which at just the right moment puts itself within my reach so that I might hang on to it and escape that embarrassing fall flat on the ground.

I sit gasping for a moment, regaining my

composure after the danger has passed; then I turn to Tamaara, and with all the love you'd expect, I say to her:

— Merci, sweetheart. A thousand thanks. How can I ever return all your favors?

I wrap my arms around her dear trunk and plant on it a kiss of gratitude. Then I take a good look around to make sure that no one has seen me, knowing full well that it is rare to find a creature who understands the true meaning of gratitude.

The thought of my guardian angel crosses my mind, that angel who loves me from afar, who looks after my best interests and watches over me, who inspires me from time to time with an idea that may at first appear to be of no value but is, in fact, very useful. Yes, the sun had been awfully hot and I was going to move of my own accord to where I could seek shelter under Tamaara's branches. But what made me move the yellow chair to just that spot, the spot next to my friend's trunk where I could grab onto it at the critical moment? Had I not done so, how would things have been, with me tipped over on the lawn in the old yellow straw chair like an upside-down bucket?

Chapter Eight

Where did the strange tree that talks come from?

The Strange Tree

Walking along the side path, I suddenly find it in a corner before me, this strange tree that I can't remember having seen here before. Gum'a hasn't asked me for money for it as he usually does whenever he brings us something, even a dried-up stick, and I haven't heard from Amina that he's asked her.

It is a tree about chest high, with a thin trunk and big flat leaves that clash strongly with its height, so that each branch carries no more than two or three. The leaves themselves are strangely colored, rebelling against everything I know about plants and their love of order and symmetry. This leaf is a dark gray-green, that one a vivid pistachio, a third is split lengthwise in two, one half an ordinary green, and the other a bright, melony orange! Another is hot pink, with strange green markings on its lower part that look like the brushstrokes of an artist on his palette.

When I see Gum'a, I say to him:

— What's this tree, Gum'a?

— It's called Akaliifa, Bey.

— Aka what?

— Akaliifa.

— Meaning?

— I don't know, Bey. That's what they call it at the nursery.

— You're the one who brought it?

— Not exactly, Bey.

— Well, then, how did it get here?

— There must have been an old cutting buried underground that came up with the hoeing. This will grow in no time; it'll be a beauty.

I don't know how I'll be able to get used to this strange name, Akaliifa. Even after its inevitable shortening to Liifa. I can't swallow the idea that it's been buried underground and come up by itself; it's just not convincing. But then again, as long as Gum'a has seen others like it at the nursery, I have to dismiss the intriguing notion that it's a tree from outer space that arrived on a little shooting star that nobody noticed. Looking at the green markings on the pink leaf, a strange feeling comes over me that this tree wants to say something to us in a language that we don't know. Yes, Liifa will do as a name for her, unless, God forbid, I am required—in that I'm writing my observations in Arabic—to take this Arabicizing to its limit and call her Aqaliifa.*

---

*In addition to a letter like the English "k," classical Arabic has another emphatic "k," often transliterated "q." This second sound is used in only a few words in Egyptian colloquial. Afifi playfully thumbs his nose here at the more formal, prestigious written language, happy to remind the reader that his garden is scandalously plebian.

Chapter Nine

A dog with a wish——a letter from our dear one——why this dizziness——a ticket around the world——the boy who doesn't know the dual form

Fido has a Sunbath
❧
Hamada's Letter and Dizziness

Isn't it comical that I have begun to worry about going up and down the four steps leading from the porch to the garden? If rheumatism were a contagious disease, I would say that it had spread from Amina's knee to mine. Once I've gotten down the stairs, I have to lift up my foot and take the widest step I can to keep from stepping on the column of ants that's always there. It is actually two columns: one of them heads from the porch stairs to the low stone border around the lawn, and the other heads back in the reverse direction. On the way, pairs of ants meet and exchange what looks like a quick kiss, and then they continue on their endless mission in silence. I don't know what they are transporting or what they spend their time on all day.

I had just gotten settled in my yellow straw chair when, at the back of the garden, I saw something rather surprising, though in reality it wasn't strange at all. After all, what's strange about a dog lying in the sun? But he is lying in my garden. How long will that stupid creature remain ignorant of the fact that it is forbidden for him to bring his uncleanness onto the pure ground of my garden?

He could see me before I saw him, but still he did not move. Now, all he does there where he lies with his neck stretched out on the grass is to lift towards me a black eye full of hope and wag his tail several times. Has the scoundrel figured out that my opinion of him differs from Amina's and that, upon seeing me, he doesn't need to leap up in fright and run like a madman?

In his humble black eyes I hear a pleading voice:

— Please, sir, let me sun myself here a couple of minutes. I know we have sun over in the shed yard, but I'm dying for some of your sun, especially with you sitting here with me, as if we were one family. By the way, sir, the missus went out a little while ago.

Now who am I to refuse all of that beseeching and to deprive this poor creature of the pleasure of the sun and society?

By God, His Master's Voice—that's how I addressed him in my mind—I'd really like to get up and bring you something to eat from the kitchen, but of course you know the rigors of the journey. The column of ants I'd have to step over, and then the four steps, and then the search in the kitchen for a pot with something you'd like in it, and then the hunt for a ladle and an old plate that could be put in front of an unclean creature such as yourself, and then the four steps again and the column of ants. And you know how your uncle has begun to suffer from the pains of rheumatism.

I imagine that I see in his eye a look of understanding, and gratitude, and a prayer for me that my house always prospers, and the assurance that he desires nothing from me but the pleasure of the sun and companionship.

Amina appears at the garden gate carrying a paper bag with the groceries she'd gone out to buy. The dog hears the creak of the gate and rushes off in fright, heading for the hole in the hedge he'd come through. Amina sees nothing but his rump just as he is disappearing. Nevertheless, she yells at him in rebuke:

— Beat it! Hope you get a bellyache!

And then to me:

— So, has your highness been entertaining him here, or what?

I don't answer her. She puts the bag on the ground, leans over, and is rooting in it for something or other.

— The mailman met me on the way and gave it to me . . . where did it go?

At last she finds the envelope she is looking for, takes it, and stands up quickly. She has hardly done so when I see her wobble and moan and hurriedly pull the green chair over to sit down on, raising her hands to press her temples and biting down on her lower lip.

— What's the matter, Amina?

She doesn't answer right away, as is her habit when she is in pain, as if to worry the person asking even more. At last she says emphatically:

— If this keeps up, I'll send for Dr. Fathi.

She is silent again, and I say insistently:

— Can't I know what's wrong?

— For the last few days, every time I bend over to do something and stand up right away, I feel dizzy, and my head pounds.

She waits a minute until the symptoms subside,

then starts prying open the envelope in her hand. She turns the paper this way and that for a minute, then pushes it toward me saying:

— See what this might be.

It turns out to be a plane ticket good for a round trip to Los Angeles. In the accompanying letter is an explanation from Hamada saying . . . "This is a ticket to Los Angeles that I got for next to nothing from an airline I joined recently, and I hope one of you will come and have a look at America. Room and board are on me, of course."

So Hamada is still Hamada, eternally ignorant of grammar, addressing his parents in the plural rather than the dual.* Another piece of news in his letter makes us very happy: the boy has left Massachusetts for California, with its brilliant sunshine and its gentle breezes. He has settled there and has a good job with an airline. So, at last, when anyone asks Amina where her son is living, she will be able to answer correctly.

---

*Written Arabic, unlike Egyptian colloquial, distinguishes between the dual and the plural. It is one of the more commonly forgotten rules, and here Hamada has neglected to make the distinction in the pronoun "you."

Chapter Ten

A sleeping little old girl—the day the boy played—the secret of the forbidden smile

The Boy Is Playing

Amina sleeps like a little girl; asleep, everyone is a child. A child of sixty, mouth open in that dopiness that characterizes human beings when they become separated from the world of consciousness. I hope her dreams are of California, or even Massachusetts, or anywhere at all except that place from whose remoteness the man came running. I hear her, near dawn, open the refrigerator and eat something from it ravenously the way she used to long ago, just after the tragedy. On her way back, she is panting for breath and talking to herself.

— May he protect you, Hamada! May he protect you! Protect you and keep you!

Then she goes back to sleep, forgetting as she seldom does, to turn out the lamp. Once, this poor old woman was a girl, beautiful, desirable, full of the will to live and full of the child whose fate it was to perish. Many long years ago, she stretched out on the couch to read, and suddenly called out to me:

— Come quick! Run! Give me your hand!

She grabbed my hand and placed it on a particular spot on her stomach, saying in utter joy:

— Do you feel him? He's playing! By God, he's playing!

It was the fetus from whom she'd been waiting for the merest sign of life for a whole month . . . I could really feel him move restlessly and twist beneath my hand, that strange creature who, deep in the shadows, was nourishing himself from her blood.

— I've got to tell Mama.

And up she jumped to let fly the happy news to family and relatives.

By the light of the lamp she has forgotten to turn out, I see two pictures of the boy we've lost. A picture of him as a baby yelling and flailing at the air with both hands, and the other as a handsome young man fighting a smile which is trying to impose itself on the picture. One day—out of compassion for her in the face of the remorselessness of the continuing memory—

I proposed to her that we move those two pictures to somewhere other than our bedroom. Her eyes lit up with a strange gleam that frightened me, and she said:

— Are you stark raving mad? Take Ibrahim's pictures away from my side? My own Ibrahim! These pictures will stay here before my eyes forever, until God gives me permission and I go to him myself!

I often catch her standing in front of the pictures for no particular reason, or sitting on the edge of the bed gazing at them, soaking them up as she murmurs prayers. And from time to time, she lifts a hand to brush away a tear that dried up long ago.

Amina coughs a dry cough and stretches out a hand, feeling for the lamp to turn it off.

Chapter Eleven

Abstaining from frogs—the goddess
doesn't sting twice

Muuny and the Frogess

There is no doubt that the nail I hammered into the back leg of the yellow straw chair has had some effect, but something to write home about, it's not, so I hope that my dear Tamaara and her solid trunk are prepared to save me again from the humiliation of a fall.

Muuny sleeps nearby, safe in my protection from unwelcome guests. At a sudden rustle from beneath the hedge, she lifts her head. I follow her gaze, and we see Froggie. Muuny, however, immediately lowers her head and goes back to sleep, regretting the effort she has expended in lifting it. Those with no garden expertise might wonder why an epicurean cat like Muuny would abstain from the meat of such a plump creature as a frogess, which, we hear, is served in the finest of European restaurants. But once upon a time, Muuny was young and inexperienced, and she fell into the same error that non-expert gardeners would.

No sooner had the young Muuny heard a similar rustle in the hedge than, announcing an attack, she flattened her stomach to the ground and gave her rump that instinctive little shake. Then off she shot like an arrow toward the target. As soon as she reached it, though, she braked to a stop and looked as though she'd decided she'd better rethink things. This creature wasn't running as all creatures do, but rather hopping, the way grasshoppers and locusts and other little creatures do. But that such behavior should come from a big animal seemed strange to her, or, at the very least, unbecoming.

She stretched out a careful, inquisitive paw and tapped twice with it on the frogess's back. When Muuny saw that she made no response, she pressed down with her paw to pin her to the ground, where she remained still, willing to cooperate with the dumb little cat right to the end. Muuny then proceeded to the final and decisive step, bringing her nose close to the frogess' back for a sniff and a little investigative lick. No sooner had she done so than she retracted her head swiftly and leapt backwards, as if she'd been electrocuted. With her paw she rubbed her nose vigorously to wipe from it some evil that had latched onto it, shaking her head violently to rid it of all traces of that evil. Had she found herself in the bathroom, I wouldn't have been surprised to see her wash her face with soap and water.

That was her reckoning from the frogess, who stayed still where she was—no doubt to make fun of the dumb cat—until she was sure that the encounter was over, then took two jumps with which she reached the shed yard, passing under the hedge.

It was a useful lesson to Muuny and to me. From a few books on the subject of animals, I learned the secret of the matter. Nature, seeing the frogess equipped neither for battle nor for flight, except in that way demeaning to animal dignity, decided to give her a special gland. When circumstances required, it would excrete a foul-smelling, foul-tasting substance, nearly poisonous to boot. The ignorant attacker had only to begin to make contact with it to bring about what had happened to dumb little Muuny.

So this little Froggie is not as innocent as his comical appearance might suggest. It seems there's no such thing as an innocent creature. I wonder if that's true as well of the nice white butterfly. He is still loafing—Froggie, that is—under the hedge. Then he takes a jump and says to me, in parting:

— Aawww!

I take a good look around myself before answering his *salaam,* from where I sit on the old yellow straw chair.

Chapter Twelve

My guardian angel, I love you—a terrible
sight on Rina's trunk—the discovery of a talent
for screaming—Rina against the truck—
a grateful branch trembles

Rina and the Guardian Angel

Once again, I feel that I should believe the story
of the guardian angel that looks out for my best interests and watches over me and protects me from so
many of life's calamities. Otherwise, what would have
prompted me that day to go out on the balcony an
hour earlier than I usually do, just at the critical
moment that separates life from death? I had just gone
out when I saw on the tall trunk behind the hedge
something so unusual it could hardly be believed. I
saw a dark man, ugly in appearance (and in significance, no doubt) hugging the graceful trunk with both
arms and legs, climbing it with the agility of a monkey. His waist was secured to it by a special belt and

in his hand was a big gleaming ax, which left no doubt as to the base deed the villain was about to perpetrate.

If I had a bad heart, I would have fallen down dead on the spot. Thank God, rheumatism is not one of those diseases that prevents a man from screaming when the need arises. From the depths of my grieving heart, I let go one scream after another that shook the garden from end to end, screams I would never have believed I was capable of as long as I lived.

— Gum'a! Gum'a! Where are you, Gum'a! You bastard, Gum'a! Gum'a! Gum'aaaa!

The doubly ugly man froze on the tall graceful trunk, and Gum'a's voice reached me from the back of the shed yard, saying in obvious amazement:

—Yes, Bey, is something the matter?

— Get over here immediately!

I saw the white tent approach from behind the hedge, and the hoarse voice asked innocently:

—What can I do for you, Bey?

I said in a voice that required all my efforts to keep it from trembling:

—What's that man doing on the tree?

Gum'a said simply:

— He's going to cut it down, sir!

I screamed at him like a madman:

—What do you mean cut it down? Does he think he can do what he pleases?

—The Hagg Zakiir is the one who ordered it, sir, on account of the new truck, that is.

And he explained to me how the contractor, owner of the property, had bought a big new tractor trailer, and how he had come the day before and tried to get into the yard with it, and how the tree had blocked the path, and he had ordered it uprooted.

— Just like that?

—That's what happened, Bey.

—Well why doesn't he widen the gate?

— It costs money to widen the gate, but cutting the tree down will bring in money!

— OK, go around and come in here to me.

Before Gum'a arrived, I had a five-pound note in the pocket of my robe, and while I spoke to him, my hand gripped it as if drawing my strength from it. I said with all the calm I could muster:

— Look, Gum'a, it so happens that this tree means something to me. You could say I've gotten used to it and it's like part of the garden.

And he said, with a ring of sadness in his hoarse voice:

— So have I, Bey, by God, but I'm just following orders.

— Well, Gum'a, don't cut it down. Just for my sake, Gum'a.

I felt a note of pleading in my voice that I didn't like, and Gum'a said in bewilderment:

— But what will I say to Hagg Zakiir?

— Tell him anything. Here.

And I held out the magic bill towards him, saying:

— Give that man his due, and keep the rest.

It seems the smell of the bill was more piercing than I had realized, as the man on the tree suddenly yelled:

— Do I start or not? Give us an idea, huh?

So Gum'a said to him:

— Come on down, 'Abdu. I'll be right over.

The man grumbled:

— Go up, 'Abdu. Come down, 'Abdu. May God relieve us of this lousy job!

Gum'a stuffed the bill into the depths of his ample pocket and went off swaying. I wish from the depths of my heart that I knew where that guardian angel was so that I might go to him and give him his due and compensate him if that were possible.

Across the hedge, I gave dear Rina—who at this

moment might have been just a big dead pile of wood on the shed yard ground—a smile and sent her a kiss on the air. And I saw one of her branches tremble, though there was no wind to move it. This, in my opinion, is as big a show of thanks as a reasonable man should expect from a casuarina tree.

Chapter Thirteen

A record stops—a woman with a cold stomach—the duty of condolences to His Master's Voice—two unclean licks, not one

---

The Death of Shahata

— Brother! Lucky you, the way you sleep! Do you mean to say you didn't hear a thing?

This is Amina's good morning to me as I sit in the robin's egg armchair that used to be blue, drinking my tea from the big brown china cup on the round table that I can't remember why or when was painted such a decisive black.

— She was wailing to high heaven!

It was Shahata's mother's voice, as Amina explains to me, when at the dawn prayer, the woman discovered that her son had stopped crying for no reason, that he wasn't moving, not even breathing or responsive to slaps. Her voice rose then, and she gathered round her some of the neighbor women. She cried for a whole hour, striking her face with both hands in lamentation, and eulogizing the dead child in her lap, until the woman whose job it was to wash the body and prepare it for burial arrived. This was the third of Gum'a's children to die, they said again. Of Gum'a, it is said that he made an attempt to analyze this fact:

— The bitch has a cold stomach; all her children come out underdone!

I decide not to go down to the garden, avoiding the sad ambience of the shed yard and the voices of the lamenters who take turns reciting stories of dead children:

— Ma'am, Hagga!

Gum'a's voice at the kitchen door. Amina goes to answer, and comes back saying:

— He needs two pounds, poor thing, so he can bury the boy.

I give her the two pounds and struggle to my feet to do the loathsome duty of paying condolences to the unfortunate man.

— May your life be long, Gum'a!

— And yours, Bey.

— Courage; it happens to us all.

— Everything is in God's hands, Bey.

Where he stands in the garden at the kitchen door I catch sight of something unusual: the dog, His Master's Voice, has come into the garden with his master for the first time. He stands there looking at us stupidly, wagging his tail. But it isn't strange that Amina should let him in that day: death has a more powerful smell than all others, even the smell of impurity. Then Gum'a excuses himself and moves off in his tent, head bowed, looking more worried about the burial than sad about the child who has died.

As for me, I don't find a single particle of sadness in my heart for the child. What I feel is closer to relief for this poor creature who is at last done repeating that rusty funereal melody that had no other word but "Aah."

Then, after a while, I take a chance on going down to the garden, as silence has settled over the shed yard, except for the cry of the chicken who is laying. I sit on the yellow straw chair listening to the silence, but after a bit am overcome by a feeling that I am under observation. And there in the nearby opening in the hedge, I see the long brown muzzle of His Master's Voice, looking at me questioningly: Can I come in? And although I don't answer, in he comes. He stops near me and wags his tail, at a loss as to what to do with himself now that he is in the forbidden garden. I feel a strong desire to touch him, while at the same time I am somewhat repelled at the idea of his impurity. But soon I laugh at myself and stretch out my hand towards him, calling:

— Come here, Fido. Come closer, here.

It is his turn to hesitate before this unprecedented overture. Then, slowly, he begins to move closer. He takes two steps and stops, then another that puts him in front of me. Towards my outstretched hand he lowers his head so that I might pet his brown hairless skull.

— Are you really impure, Fido?

That's what I ask him, and he emits a soft, unintelligible whine. Then I add:

— May your life be long, Master.

He wags his tail so hard then that his whole rear end dances, and by way of returning my condolences, he inclines his head and furtively plants on the back of my hand two sticky licks with his long, black, impure tongue.

Chapter Fourteen

Don't worry too much about your wife—
what about the ticket?—the old woman
and the coiffeur and jasmine tea

Amina in Bed and Jasmine Tea

All my life I have worried when Amina got sick, even with a trivial illness. I understood it to be because of my great love for her and my concern for her welfare, until one day a miserable psychiatrist told me that excessive worry over a sick person is nothing but an unconscious attempt to hide a secret wish that the sickness be terminal. Of course this upset me, but I dismissed it on the grounds that it was an unconscious desire among a certain ilk of psychiatrists to distort all noble motives and to spoil the moods of those who had them.

But I am excused if I worry about her these days because of that dizziness that has become her almost daily visitor. We call in Dr. Fathi, the short, thin man, calm almost to the point of coldness, the family doctor for years. With his great precision and his typical patience, he examines her and eliminates by his methods those illnesses that should be eliminated. Then he says in a neutral voice:

— Your blood pressure's a little high; ease off on salty foods. And I'd like you to take a test for diabetes.

The diabetes test comes back negative, so he orders her to follow a healthy diet for a week with bed rest and some medication.

At this point, Amina says to me when she sees me sitting motionless before her:

— Now why are you tying yourself to my side like this? Get up and go down to your garden and sit by your trees!

She pulls out a pad of paper and a pencil and says:

— I'm going to write a letter to my dear Hamada.

She has just started writing when a look of consternation comes over her and she says:

— But what will I tell him about the plane ticket?

I suggest to her that she write to him about the difference between the plural and the dual when addressing one's parents. Ignoring me, she says:

— Really, what should I say?

—What should you tell him? Tell him thanks but no thanks, not today!

Maliciously, she says:

— I'll just tell him to send another. You might take it into your head to take me and go!

I say sarcastically:

— Me travel to America? I have a hard enough time traveling to the far end of the garden!

I get up and feel a twinge in my knee as if I'd gone up the stairs.

— I'll be sitting right here on the balcony if you need anything.

I leave her chewing distractedly on the pencil, a stumped pupil of sixty. On the balcony I sit on the red straw chair, after cleaning the jasmine blossoms off it. It is late afternoon, and I don't like late afternoon; I'd rather spend it sleeping. It reminds me of nothing more than an old woman who goes to the beauty parlor every day and comes back to sit in front of me, trying to tell from my eyes what my opinion is. And my opinion is one that will always disappoint her and throw across the wrinkles of her face a yellow like the yellow of this late afternoon. The shadows of the trees have begun to lengthen and overlap, darkening the garden early, and the tall, graceful, harmonious tree is clothed in a sad yellow veil.

On my side, a jasmine flower falls into the brown china cup and floats to the surface of the tea, like a lotus flower on the surface of a sacred lake. Amina, like many others, likes to drink tea with mint. Why shouldn't I be the first to try it with jasmine?

Chapter Fifteen

Why didn't the cat eat the lizard?——food for
beautiful children——charming, tender mothers

The Cat and the Lizard

Muuny is lying on her side licking her white chest
and what she can reach of her stomach, the way she
did in her youth, in the last days of her pregnancy,
when she wanted to prepare her six nipples for the
cherished kittens she was expecting. Today, of course,
she's aiming for nothing more than general cleanliness.

I saw her, in just this pose, nurse four kittens of
different colors, attached to her chest and stomach
like big greedy worms bent on devouring her.
Unresisting, happy, she reached with her tongue from
time to time to lick the kittens' backs and clean them.
Another interpretation would say, cleanliness nothing! She was out to benefit from the vitamin B that is
so abundant in the kittens' coats.

For some reason, she saw fit to put an end to the

nursing and get up, escaping with difficulty from the worms clinging to her body. Hurrying towards the hedge, she left them there in the corner, looking at me and meowing as if to say:

— Take care of the kids!

She hadn't been in the shed yard for more than a few moments before she came leaping energetically back. Dangling from her mouth was something long and squirming whose identity might confound those with no garden expertise. Experts, however, would recognize it immediately as a fat lizard, half alive. Non-experts might wonder why the cat didn't eat that lizard. Experts would tell them that she had not hunted it to eat it, but for the sake of the beautiful children, for whom mother's milk was no longer sufficient and for whose health a varied diet had become a necessity.

She headed back with the lizard and deposited it before them. They came sniffing to examine it. It was apparently the first lizard they had inspected in their lives. The banquet pleased them and they began to tear it apart and eat, with the tender mother standing to watch, it never crossing her mind to reach out a paw for a single morsel. It was a truly touching picture of the tenderness that characterizes Muuny despite her many other ignominies.

I could hardly forget the other tender mother, the lizard, that is, whom I am sure only left the nest to get something to feed her beautiful children. A tender mother found herself, in a moment of bad luck, in the mouth of another slightly larger, tender mother. But it all evens out in the end, as long as it happens in the lap of the great tender mother, their mother, the earth.

I stretch out my hand towards Muuny to stroke her white stomach and say teasingly:

—You better not have gone and gotten pregnant in your old age!

She looks at me reprimandingly, as if to say:

— What rot! Can I even eat, much less get pregnant?!

Chapter Sixteen

Clean, nervous days—about dust and jasmine—jasmine in the garbage—the puzzle of the perfumed poison—the dear idiot

---

Jasmine on the Carpet

Because she is tall and graceful, she has to be the one who suffers most from that despicable wind they call the *xamasiin*. When those winds blow through Zahiira and Tamaara, they are tolerable, and those two only lose a few leaves. The *xamasiin*'s real power, though, is at the tips of the high trees. It batters them, bending them from side to side. From the angle at which they lean, they look as though their roots might snap at any moment from this springtime abuse. If winter is hard on people abroad, it compensates by giving us a hard time in spring, almost depriving us of it entirely. If our poets sing of the gentle breezes of spring, they are nothing more than parrots repeating what the poets who actually have a spring say. They turn a blind eye to the dusty wind that coats every-thing in a dismal yellow and makes eyes even blinder than they already are.

I open the door of the balcony, and a powerful gust of rather hot wind strikes me, but I want to experience it. Inside, I sit on the robin's egg armchair that used to be blue, looking at the floor of the balcony that the wind has covered with fallen jasmine flowers. Another strong gust blows a bunch of these blossoms into the room, decorating the old wine-colored carpet with fragrant white circles. I hear a banging and slamming of windows and furniture from a distance: as Amina had been resting for a whole week, she has to compensate with an entire day of fierce cleaning. With her big, fearsome dust beater, she begins whacking everything weak and helpless, chairs and whatnot, in her path. Here comes the banging down the long hallway. As soon as Amina appears in the door of the room and sees the floor, she strikes her chest with her hand.

— Oh, no!! How did that mess get in here?

I say, mockingly:

— Now I've heard everything: jasmine flowers are a mess.

Ignoring my remark, she says:

—You've got the door wide open!

She hurries off to the little hall that leads to the kitchen, disappearing for a moment, then reappearing carrying a broom with a long wooden handle and a scoop. With the broom, she pushes the jasmine mess towards the scoop with an unaccustomed agility from which all the symptoms of rheumatism are absent. Having finished scooping up all the jasmine, she heads for the balcony door, sarcastically asking my permission:

— May I please close it?

She has already done so, muttering:

— He can't be separated from his trees for a single day!

I make no comment, having learned from experience to ignore her little barbs as much as I can on clean days like this. Scoop in hand, she heads for the kitchen, where the jasmine will find its sad end in the garbage can.

I remember a study I read in some magazine or other whose validity I'm not sure of, about the girls whose profession it is to gather the jasmine harvest on the big farms year after year, and how all of them die before they're thirty for mysterious reasons. These reasons, nevertheless, are perfectly clear: the girls' relationship to the jasmine. The sweet intoxicating smell of jasmine is not as innocent as it might seem. It is actually a deadly poison to those who ingest it for a long time. Year after year, the aromatic poison works its way into the chests of the poor girls, where it makes its nest, gradually leaching into their blood to deal them that slow death. In the depths of the dark, decaying grave, I wonder how long the perfume of the jasmine emanates from the body of a girl who died for its sake . . .

A strong gust of wind opens the door which Amina has closed, sullying the wine-colored carpet again with the laughing blossoms. I sigh and get up to gather them, and in the palm of my hand I lift them to my nose to inhale their perfume before putting them into the pocket of my gray robe. Yes, they'll wilt there and die, but perhaps my pocket is a somewhat more honorable grave for them than the garbage can.

I close the balcony door, as it had been, and stand behind the glass, saying to my friends in apology:

— Sorry, beauties, forgive me today.

From behind, I hear Amina's voice saying in surprise:

—Who are you talking to?

I answer her succinctly:

—The trees, of course.

I wait for her usual retort about my brain and its endowment, but she makes none. Instead, in a tone so innocent it seems naive, she says:

— Can the trees hear you with the door closed?

Despite an effort, I find myself shaking with a smothered laugh, and I go over to her and, on the wrinkles of her cheek, plant a kiss of love.

—What is that for?

That's what she asks me in her surprise, and I answer honestly:

— I love you.

Chapter Seventeen

A murderous desire—is she praying—a humble bride—love without a head—he loves and she has lunch—food of the elite—the last look of death—the apologizing snake

---

The Praying Mantis

On the foliage of nearby Jasmine, I see something which provokes in me, quite out of the ordinary, a strong desire to kill. That long piece of dried-out green has given itself away with a little movement. Its head is triangular, like a bicycle seat, and its arms are sharp, like saws, and from time to time it lifts its hands up on either side of its head and moves them; the naive observer might imagine it is praying.

— I want to get up and kill her!

That's what I say to Amina as we sit on the balcony one morning when the wind died down.

—Who?

—That criminal.

I pointed to the praying mantis, and Amina's eyes comb the green until she sees her and says:

— *Haraam!* She's holy.

And where she sits on the green chair which I'd moved to the balcony, she explains to me that there is a religious opinion of some weight that affirms that the Prophet, peace be upon Him, had ridden one of her kind to Jerusalem on his midnight journey.*

—Would you like me to tell you what I saw this holy thing do?

And before she can answer with a yes or a no, I begin telling her how this little green tramp lies in wait, just as she's doing now, for the poor, unsuspecting groom. She knows that he has only to arrive in order to fall into the trap into which many others preceded him. Having arrived, just a few moments of shyness elapse before he finds himself in the natural position for the task, namely, on her back. Everything is beautiful so far.

---

*Orthodox Islam teaches that the Prophet made a midnight journey to the seven heavens, called Laylat al-'Israa', on the back of the miraculous horse, Al Boraaq. The journey is said to have begun from Jerusalem, hence the city's revered status. The name of the praying mantis is *faras an-nabi,* literally "the Prophet's Horse." Hence this popular, but not orthodox, belief.

God has given this bride a singular talent in the animal kingdom: her amazing ability to twist her neck backwards and give her head a complete rotation, so that, as popular comics say, her face is where the nape of her neck should be.* She turns that hellish instrument around slowly until her face is directly opposite the groom's. This might suggest to the poetically inclined observer—as it has suggested to more than one groom—that, at the height of passion, she longs to plant a hot kiss on the groom's mouth.

But kisses, as it becomes apparent shortly, are the last thing this green tramp has in mind. No. She is instinctively searching her groom's neck for a particular gland whose function is the suppression of the sex drive in ordinary circumstances, that gland which under the present circumstances has become an impediment that must be done away with. With the skill of a surgeon, she carves a slit in his neck that leads to the gland, and then she begins nibbling on it with the greatest tenderness, so as not to injure the intoxicated groom's feelings.

---

*The nape of the neck, *il 'afa,* in Egyptian colloquial, being the chosen spot on which to cuff a person, already has a humorously derogatory connotation.

And from that gland, she moves on to his neck, and with the same tenderness and elegance, she nibbles away until she finishes it off, until the groom has lost a relatively important organ for living creatures, namely his head.

The nervous system in these creatures is not a central system as it is in us. Instead, each of the nodes that makes up the body contains an independent nerve center that can function of its own accord without relying on the head.

Therefore, it often happens that the groom pursues his romantic function for a long time without a head. He is up to his ears, loving the lady. She is utterly oblivious to this, however, busy as she is consuming him leisurely, a piece at a time. In short, he's making love and she's having lunch. And once he has exhausted his objectives as groom, she throws him off her back and onto the ground and opens his stomach, searching for any tasty morsels that might be there by way of dessert.

— See, dear, your holy creature?

Amina doesn't answer right away, absorbed as she is in counting the blue stitches on the knitting needles, her eyes drawn in over her nose, making her almost cross-eyed. At last she asks:

— Where'd you hear that?

— From books.

She says decisively:

— Don't believe everything you read in books!

And before I can object, she adds:

— Now please let me count these stitches!

She goes on counting, and I go on observing that evil green thing and chewing on my murderous thoughts.

Then comes a rustle from under the hedge, and a body jumps twice. From my position on the balcony, I can't see Froggie's eyes, but I hear him say:

— Aaaww!

There is a note of hesitation in his voice, too, because he can't see me either from there. A third jump hides him from me in the shed yard, and my mind jumps to a day when I'd been at the zoo, and I'd found myself in front of a big glass house where they kept one of the giant snakes. In a corner, the snake was lying all coiled up like a rope that sailors had piled up on the pier, to tow a ship with, should the need arise. He was sound asleep, the innocence of a nursing infant in his open black eyes. He had eaten, gotten full, and gone to sleep. When he woke up hungry, he had only to stretch his head to a pond right there in the cage, inhabited by a tribe of frogs of all different sizes. The frogs ate what they found in the stagnant water, living in a strange, calm indifference to the terrible danger lurking beside them all the time.

So the snake woke up and stretched his head toward the pond to examine them, choosing from among them what looked good for his meal. For a moment, his black eyes met the two protruding eyes of a frogess in the strangest look that two creatures can exchange before one eats the other. In the eyes of the snake, I looked for hatred but didn't find it, nor any sense of sin. And in the eyes of the frogess, I found no fear, not even any reproach. And while I was looking into the eyes of the snake, I imagined I heard him say to the frogess:

— I'm very sorry, sister, for what I'm about to do, but you know that this is the law of life. For me to live, you must die. I wish they'd put a nice fat rat or a satisfying little pig in instead of you. But being as there's nothing else before me, I'll just have to eat you. I don't imagine you'd want to make a scandal of me among my peers and have me be the first snake in history to die because he'd gone on a hunger strike for moral considerations.

I would have liked to hear the frogess' answer to that speech, but the scoundrel didn't give her a chance.

Gardens will always be the best place for a thoughtful person to spend his time as long as they contain, in addition to trees and flowers and birds and cats, frogs with inquiring bulging eyes. This is a truth unchanged by the far-off, endless, background whine of a record stuck on the word "Aah."

Chapter Eighteen

The endless column——the ant killer in hell——
bulk and retail in killing ants——watch out
for the ants, Gum'a

Ants and My Mother and Gum'a

I have, of course, stepped on it more than once without realizing, the ant column that's always busy at the porch steps. I would realize it when I felt the crunch underfoot, look, and see dozens of ants speeding this way and that in a state of unforeseen chaos, besides those writhing on the ground, crushed beneath my hulking foot. Nevertheless, the greater part of the column was still marching as if nothing had happened, passing by the writhing ants without even looking at them, or looking at them and not seeing them, or seeing them and not showing any concern at what had happened. For them, it's a daily event, no more, no less, one of the familiar dangers in the ant business.

Once upon a time, when I was a child, I would

see an ant walking and whack it with my foot, killing it with outright premeditation. I felt that I was exercising a right and carrying out a duty, killing that lowly creature that would so brazenly cross the path of such a mighty creature as myself.

One day my mother saw me and gave me a proper tongue-lashing. She told me what humiliation awaited cruel people like me on Judgment Day, and of the subsequent torment of hellfire, where the wicked burn eternally. This talk filled me with dread, and I renounced once and for all the killing of ants. I would even walk with my head bent towards my footsteps, lest I unintentionally kill a poor wayward ant.

Then, one day I saw my mother pick up a big bottle from which emanated the smell of kerosene. She headed with it for a corner of the kitchen where she squatted to empty its contents into one of the holes there.

— What are you doing, Mama?

Such was my innocent question, but she did not answer, as it became clear that she was pouring the kerosene into an ants' nest with the intention of exterminating them and cleansing the kitchen of them. I was utterly amazed at the glaring inconsistency before me: my mother deemed it permissible for her to kill thousands of ants in one fell swoop, while she called me to account for my innocent enjoyment, from time to time, of killing one lone ant. Didn't she care about the painful torment that awaited her on Judgment Day? Or could it be that she knew—without telling me—that killing ants wholesale was permissible, whereas only killing them retail is forbidden? Or was it more serious than that? Did God Almighty have double standards, permitting big strong mothers what he forbid to poor, helpless, little children?

I set about directing a lot of such questions to my mother who listened for a while in silence to take them in. When she had, she said to me shortly:

— Go play outside!

The sound of water gushes from the hose onto the ground of the garden behind the house. Then Gum'a's back appears after a while, pulling the hose along the ground, pointing it here and there as the watering requires. Even the sand path needs to be sprinkled to keep the sand in place, and here he is just a meter away from the column.

—Watch the ants, Gum'a!

That's what I am about to yell at him, but I hold

my tongue at the last minute, since a remark like that would be enough to arouse in Gum'a the greatest astonishment, to the point where he might even doubt my mental faculties. I could well become the laughing-stock of the neighborhood for a long time. The ants, whatever their significance, aren't mammals or birds or other vertebrates to which I'm related. So why should I make a mockery of myself for an animal to which no direct biological link ties me?

I do no more than turn my face away when he reaches the column with the hose, imagining hundreds of them plastered to the ground or flying through the air before the violent stream of water. I look at Gum'a's face and find him smiling, happily moving the hose right and left. As if it were a machine gun, he aims it at the column of those who disagree with him. And those he does not kill with the water, he kills with his big clump-ing bare feet and with the hose he pulls along behind him on his destructive round of irrigation.

I sigh in resignation and keep quiet; what can I do? Shall we let the garden die of thirst for the sake of the ants and the other little crawling things that the water drowns? What makes it more bearable for me is that none of the inhabitants of the garden pay any attention to what has happened. Not one of Tamaara's branches move, not one lemon falls from Zahiira, not a smile leaves the face of the laughing monkey in the pansy bed. So why should I be the only one to shoulder all the responsibility?

Gum'a moves off with the hose, and the sound of the water recedes with him. And from the back of the shed yard come the cries of the new child who is snuggled in his mother's lap, who has arrived to be raised, instead of Shahata, in Gum'a's care. His crying, so far, is just crying; it has not yet become that broken record, stuck on the word "Aah."

Chapter Nineteen

"Don't go out," meaning "go out"—how do
you know that thing's dead?—when I felt that
I hated Amina—a rifle of the brand
"His Master's Voice"

Fido's Death

Seeing me going down the four steps to the garden, Amina says to me:

— You're better off not going out on the sidewalk! Take your walk inside today!

What she says amazes me, of course.

— Why? What's on the sidewalk?

— I've done my duty and told you!

She quickly disappears from the balcony door before I can continue interrogating her. It is obvious that this is a frank invitation for me to go out onto the sidewalk. She would not have said this to me unless she had been afraid that I would content myself with a walk in the garden. I don't see anything unusual at first. The sidewalk is the same old sidewalk on the same little quiet street. Then my sight shifts left towards the shed yard gate a few yards opposite the garden gate, and I see that brown heap over there on the ground. Towards it I go, only to make out the body of His Master's Voice. It is quieter than a sleeping dog should be, its limbs flung about it in disarray. They could not belong to anything other than a dead dog. Yes, Fido is dead, the bullet hole that did him in clearly visible in his side, flies collecting on the congealed blood around the wound.

It is a picture of true quietude, quietude the meaning of which man can only grasp when looking at a dead creature: the no-pulse, no-motion, no-existence of any sort at all, the creature that has suddenly been transformed from the life of pulsing cells to the life of mute, cryptic atoms. It would be all the same to him now if I poured kerosene on him and set him on fire, or brought a kitchen cleaver and chopped him into little cutlets for the cats of the neighborhood, because he's simply not here. Fido is nothing more than the negative form of a dog that was.

Thank God I let him come in and sun with me, so that the poor thing didn't die with a grudge against me. He knew that I really wanted to feed him, if it hadn't been for the trip to the kitchen that I described to him. That morning I granted him some of the love he missed and made him feel that he wasn't as impure as people accused him of being.

— See what they done, sir?

It is Gum'a's voice, as he comes up behind me. His face wears an expression of greater sadness than I saw on it the day his son Shahata died.

In real anger, I say to him:

—Who's the son of a bitch who'd kill a poor dog like this?

— People with no morals, God spare you, are all over the place. God guide you, Abdallah.

—Abdallah who?

—The garbage man, to take him in his truck.

He moves the hem of his *galabiyya,* which sets the flies gathered on the wound in motion around us. With difficulty, I restrain myself from saying to him: may you have a long life, Gum'a! Inside, Amina meets me and says in a tone that is not without a trace of malice:

— I told you not to go out!

I say to her in anger:

—You look a little happy!

—What's to be happy about?

—An impure dog, and you're rid of him!

—Well, as long as you realize that, why are you upset?

This is one of the times when I try very hard not to hate Amina. That night, between sleep and waking, I hear the sound of a shot from inside the shed yard, and it seems to me that the rifle that had been fired had a rather hoarse voice.

Chapter Twenty

An attempt at identifying the tree—
Akaliifa's disappearance—ha'w with 'aw

Who Is the Tree?

Yes, I like to talk to trees from time to time. As a matter of fact, I can say I'm proud of it, and I'm amazed by those deviants who hold this beautiful, creative hobby against me. There's just one thing that bothers me as I engage in my hobby. It's that voice that keeps pestering me:

—Where is it, and who is it, this tree you're talking to, sir?

When I talk to the tree, I turn my gaze to the big green mass of its leaves. At this point, the questioner rephrases his question:

— Do you think, sir, that the tree is its leaves?

I say no, of course, because I am sure that the tree is not—as I once had actually imagined—its leaves. After all, the leaves get old and yellow. They wither and fall to the ground to be trodden underfoot with a sad crunching, while the tree itself remains standing, trunk and branches intact. True, the tree is bare of leaves, but it's not terribly concerned about this bareness.

My questioner continues with veiled sarcasm:

— Well, then, is it its trunk and branches?

I ignore his sarcasm and say no again, since I know that these are no more than the wooden skeleton, analogous to our bony one, and the assembly of pipes that transports food to the real unknown tree.

— Would you say then (my questioner continues with his sarcasm) that the tree is its blossoms and its fruit?

I am tempted to say yes, but once again I deny it: when I filled my stomach with the juice of her lemons, did I eat Zahiira up? And did I rob Tamaara of anything when, just at sunset, I filled my lungs with her intoxicating perfume?

— There's nothing left, then, but that the tree is its roots, wouldn't you say?

But of course I know that the roots are no more than talons to stabilize the tree in the earth and straws for the nutritious juices with which the depths of the earth overflow. Here the interrogator's voice reaches the height of his sarcasm, and he says:

—Well, then, sir, you talk to trees without knowing who they are?

At this point, I lose my temper and reply:

— Do I take it from these haughty questions that you know who the tree is?

He hesitates for a moment before answering, and then says with a vulgar little laugh:

— Haa 'aw 'aw ha' 'aw.

Or maybe it was:

— Haa 'aw 'aw ha' ha.'

And since I don't think there is a significant difference between the two, I forget the entire matter. Then one day as I am strolling, my feet lead me to where Akaliifa stood, in the hopes that she might have found a way to articulate what it is she wanted to say. And there a great surprise is awaiting me: Akaliifa is no longer there at all! It is as if the earth has opened up and swallowed her, leaving nothing but a dry, knee-high stick of wood stuck in the ground. Not far away, I see a big pile of bright colors that amounts to Liifa's leaves, cut off along with the branches that carried them and with more than half of her trunk, all thrown in the corner and waiting for Uncle Abdallah's cart.

For a minute, I think Gum'a has been taken by a

sudden bout of madness and cut down the tree, so I yell for him through the hedge until he answers, and I ask:

— Are you the one who cut Liifa down?

But he doesn't know the tree's name and he says:

— Liifa what, Bey?

Correcting myself, I say:

— I mean the Akaliifa tree. Are you the one who cut it down like this?

Laughing at my ignorance, he says:

— I didn't cut it down, Bey, I pruned it. So it'll grow and branch and be pretty.

Angrily, I say:

— It had branches, and it was pretty.

— No, Bey, it'll have five, six times as many branches. Just be a little patient with it, Bey, it'll be a humdinger.

Jokingly, I say:

— I thought it might have upset the Hagg somehow or other and he told you to cut it down!

Uncomprehendingly, he says:

—The Hagg?

—Yeah, maybe he went to park the truck and the tree got in his way!

Gum'a doesn't answer, having a hard time understanding, but he has given me incontrovertible evidence that I could cut all the branches off a tree with all their leaves and most of the trunk and nevertheless not have cut down the tree!

Liifa did not die, as I imagined she would, or perhaps she died and was reborn. Out of the very heart of the wood of that dry stalk green leaves began to sprout again, small at first, but shouting with life. There is something in the heart of the tree that—however badly its limbs are torn—has sworn a solemn oath to survive. It is something I don't think I will ever succeed in knowing, neither I nor that bastard who makes fun of me with his annoying questions.

— I say to Tamaara as I pat her trunk:

— Would it be such a big deal, Tamtam, if you were to tell me who you are?

Not a twig budges, not even a leaf, and I turn to Zahiira without much hope:

— Not you, either, Zuzu?

To her, as well, it is as if I've said nothing. From the pansy bed the little white body of the nice white butterfly darts away. With the whir of her departing wings, I imagine I hear the echo of a voice saying:

— Haa 'aw ha' ha' 'aw.

Chapter Twenty-One

A breath of perfume straight from Paradise—
a prayer from a lady at sunset—did she eat a
bee in love?—a many-colored banquet—
a final warning—the day of the great fall

The Great Fall

This time just before sunset is Tamaara's favorite to reveal her hidden treasures. She diffuses in all directions the most fragrant of her perfume gems. Tamaara's scent prickles the nose the way honey prickles the mouth, and lo, the whole garden is a lake of honey and musk. Even Muuny is drawn by the scent, and she comes and sits under the tree sniffing the air, hearkening to what faint peeping of birds remains.

In her gray dress, Amina comes out onto the balcony, walking slowly, holding the long *sibha* with the little black beads. As does the cat, so does Amina: she lifts her nose to fill her lungs with the pure, piquant perfume, and a pleased smile traces itself on her lips. Amina, after all, is sure that the scent of the *tamarhinna* tree, especially, is nothing other than a breath of perfume from Paradise.

Across the grass she comes, over to the green chair where she sits to continue her murmured prayers. In the waning light above us comes the sad song of the plover. For a while, its traces reverberate before they dissolve, high up in the treetops.

Then comes the sound of a bird alighting on one of Zahiira's branches. No, actually it's two birds. A heated conversation ensues between the two, a quarrel not suitable for this quiet moment redolent of the scent of Paradise. Muuny's lips and whiskers quiver as they usually do under such circumstances. Her whole body tenses in silent predatory alert. Since the dawn of time, cats have learned to love this particular avian tone, which so often announces the fall of one of the combatants. One day, while she was still young, Muuny heard this tone while she was sitting here where she sits now. In an instant she was transformed from a cat into an arrow, scampering up the trunk and through the branches. In a moment she was back with her quarry, one of the birds, snatched from the heat of battle. That, of course, was long ago. Today, her whiskers just quiver, and she can only meow bitterly.

Patches of color move across the sky, and a beautiful whispered chirping issues from them. A flock of doves who are not doves always appears in summer at this time, just before sunset. The birds wheel this way and that, flying like a squadron of planes on exhibition day, and with their turns, their color shifts from white to orange to green. One day, I asked Gum'a the name of these birds, and he said, simply:

— That's the warwaar, Bey.

I asked him suspiciously:

— What do you mean, warwaar?

— Because it warwars, Bey, can't you hear it?

Here I'd thought it was chirping, while in fact it was warwarring. And in a small guide book on birds, I actually came across an entry for a bird called "warwaar" with the characteristics of this bird, sometimes called the bee-eater. It wasn't flying to such heights for romance or devotion, as I had imagined, but rather for a snack before bedtime. It knows that the bees have preceded it, hoping to mate far from the disturbances of earthly creatures. There, in the silent heights, as it wheels about, the hungry warwaar devours all the passionate bees who cross its path.

I have heard a lot about the prayer of a woman at sunset,* but this is the first time I've seen it answered with my own eyes. At the far end of the garden, I hear a muffled sound of something striking the ground. There I see a small body jump, trying to fly, and fall, jump again, and then fall, its color changing from white to green to orange. Suddenly Muuny is no longer by my side. She is more like a whale who's dived into the sea beside me, and surfaced over there by the fallen warwaar. In the next instant, that array of colors is a single smudge between her teeth. Then, like an arrow, she shoots off into some hidden corner of the garden behind the house. Without seeing her, I imagine her teeth at work, plucking the green and orange feathers, then sinking into the soft warm flesh just fallen from the sky in whose depths lay an additional treat of fresh bees. I would find a lot of colored feathers the next day on the ground, and maybe a bill and two legs, without the warwaar to whom all those things belong. The warwaar had flown up high to eat fresh bees, and to the earth it fell so that Muuny might eat fresh warwaar. Muuny can't be blamed for being

*A rhyming proverbial saying *(Da'wit il wiliyya fii saa'it il maghribiyya)* that asserts that a woman's prayers are more likely to be answered around sunset.

a cat. She's nothing but a lady who asked the heavens for a bird that chirped, and who was given a warwaar that warwarred. It can't be expected of her, before she eats the bird, that she slaughter it and drain its blood, those procedures specific to civilized creatures like myself.

In the nearby mosque the microphone sounds the call to sunset prayer, and Amina gets up to answer it. She stops, though, when she hears Gum'a's hoarse voice through the hedge.

— Good evening, Bey. I've got some news you're not going to like, but I've got to deliver it just the same.

My heart skips a beat at this tone that I am not used to hearing from Gum'a.

— I swear on my honor, Bey, I almost lost my job yesterday. The Hagg came, just like last time, and he tried to get the truck in the driveway and couldn't . . .

He pauses, and I say in exasperation:

— Come on, out with it.

Succinctly, he says:

— The tree is going to be cut down tomorrow, Bey. I just came to let you know. I hate to be the one to tell you.

I look at Amina and see that she has fastened her

gaze on me to see how I look having heard what I've heard, and she must see a truly sad sight, which is, nevertheless, destined in an instant to become comical. As I stamp my feet against the ground and lean back in the chair, suddenly I lose my balance and launch into a new trip earthwards, still sitting on the old yellow straw chair. I rush toward the good earth and smack into it, after a futile attempt to catch hold of Tamaara's trunk as I did the last time.

Whenever I fall, I always like to get up in a hurry. It seems, though, that the world has changed. When I try to move my legs to right the chair, I am completely unable to. Neither the left leg obeys me nor the right. I just manage to lift myself up to the point where I can lean on my elbows when I see Amina put her *sibha* on the green chair and hurry over to rescue me. She leans over to grasp me under the arms and help me up. Quickly and forcefully she pulls me up. But, no sooner has she done so than her grip loosens and she lets me fall back. She lifts her hands to press her temples, moaning in pain in a muffled voice. She reaches behind herself, feeling for the green chair, but only finds an edge. Trying to sit down, she slips from it to the ground, she and the black *sibha*.

She falls to a sitting position, then topples over onto her side on the grass, curled up, trembling. After a bit, I manage to extricate myself from my predicament with the yellow chair, and I hurry to her, bending over to see what is the matter. I find a body cold as ice, drenched in sweat, shuddering on the ground the way the fallen warwaar shuddered just a little while ago.

Chapter Twenty-Two

The End

Of course I'd like to see her now, fluttering before me, the white butterfly that visits the garden every day, but it is foolish to demand of life that she change her system to accommodate the whim of an old man like me. That butterfly comes only in the morning while the sun fills the air with her warmth and her light, so what would bring her now when the sun is about to set? It's bees who are on the wing at this hour. They mate up on the silent heights, and the warwaar pursues them. It eats as many of the infatuated bees as it can, all to the sound of a song by the plover, which dissolves in the tops of the tall trees. And I don't think the plover, in turn, has flown and sung for a much nobler reason than that for which the warwaar warwarred.

Here on the porch, on the yellow straw chair, after I have cleansed it of jasmine dust, I've allowed myself to pour a little bit of Omar al-Khayyam* red

---

*An Egyptian brand.

wine into the brown pottery cup. This I allow myself before—as the one for whom the wine was named said—the balance of fate overflows the cup of life. The cup is on the porch's stone wall, where it's pleasant to sit on these hot nights as a tired breeze blows from time to time, a breeze that doesn't get lost right away among the tree branches. How pleasant it is here where Yasmina's refined breaths mingle with Tamaara's dissolute ones in a judicious balance. Looking at Tamaara, whose features have begun to disappear in the dimming light, I find I must admit that my heart is not yet completely reconciled towards her.

Yes, I know that there are no standards of any kind that would allow me to throw the responsibility on a tree for everything that happened to me and Amina weeks ago. However, we also have to consider the fact that Tamaara has never been, in all her days, just a tree. No, she has been a friend, with all the meanings the word implies, and a person expects of her everything one friend expects from another, especially in times of need. So where was my friend—or at least where was her trunk—at the time of that tragic fall that befell us while we were sitting beneath her, under her protection?

What's worse, I can't even blame that creature who was the prime reason and the essential agent of the whole tragedy, the old yellow straw chair. For a moment, I decided to blame him, when suddenly I heard from his direction a loud cry:

— People! Leave some mercy in your hearts! It's a sin, Muslims! Twenty years I've been carrying you on my back and I haven't said boo, and that's still not good enough? Twenty years I've put up with you morning, afternoon, and night, until, before its time, my health has been ruined. And now you come to tell me I'm to blame? Salt in your eye, tyrant! How could you be so cold-blooded?

I reined my blame right in, understanding his feelings, and as gently as I could, I pulled him up off the ground and patted his back. I may even have kissed him. Then I tried to get him to gather up his strength and exercise his former employment as a chair, but he announced his utter inability to carry out any of the functions of a chair, even if I didn't insist on straw or yellow. I had hardly let him go when he shuddered and fell like a dead man onto the green grass that was laughing at his failure. I couldn't think of anything to do other than prop his back against the trunk of

Tamaara and leave him there like a scarecrow, pretending to be a living creature. And so that he wouldn't feel lonely, next to him I left Amina's green straw chair, that no longer found anyone to use it, all because of the mistake of that scoundrel of a doctor who looks more like a rat.

Amina insisted on having a doctor's consultation, so Dr. Fathy brought specialists to her, colleagues whom he trusted. One of them was a fat, dark, jovial character, who said to Amina as he examined her:

— I like what I see, Hagga. I wish my health were as good as yours!

They asked for every kind of X-ray and lab test imaginable, and gathered around to examine her. Then Dr. Fathy said:

— Thank God, there's nothing of what we were worried about.

And the fat doctor backed him up, saying:

— Congratulations, Hagga, innocent on all charges!

Here the third rat-like doctor intervened, with his sallow dark face and his protruding mustache. He laughed a dry, undoctorly laugh and said sarcastically:

— Heh heh, according to the machines, that is!

Neither of his colleagues commented on his remark, and he realized his mistake and switched to English. Then they filled out a prescription with the names of medicines that covered the front and the back of the paper. With a stubbornness that pleased me, she said:

— Can't I at least know what you're treating me for?

So they told her that her overwrought nerves hadn't found any other way to express themselves than this dizziness that she complained of, and that, with medication and bed rest and a healthy diet, it would be just a matter of days before she regained her health and was as strong as a horse.

— Sii tiss! Sii tiss! Sii tiss!

A field cricket sends out a short inquisitive chirp, and when no other cricket responds, he feels ashamed of himself and falls silent.

— Krrrrrr! Krrrrrr! Krrrrrr!

So comes old Muuny's voice, as she reads nearby. Amina insists that they're readings of a religious nature, thereby establishing that the goddess Basiit is still living amongst us, a smaller divinity serving the goddess of magic, Isis.

— Sii tiss! Sii tiss! Sii tiss!

Another chirp, as the cricket tries his luck, if it is the same cricket. This time he's no sooner let it out than a chorus of cricket voices sings out in harmony. There are a few at first, then tens, then hundreds, then thousands: the cricket's common mind, having decided that all the individuals would suddenly cooperate in singing the same song in unison.

God damn that doctor once again. Amina's gaze wanders over the white sheets as she fingers the long black *sibha*. She suddenly stops her prayers, asking me:

— Didn't he say that it was according to their machines?

Playing dumb, I say:

— Who do you mean?

— The doctor.

She describes him to a tee, leaving no room for doubt as to his identity, and then goes on where she had left off:

— So maybe those machines of theirs are wrong.

I make no comment as she continues:

— So I might have something that doesn't show up on their machines!

I remain stubbornly silent; I even leave the room

on some pretext or other, though I know from my experience of her that Amina will not drop the matter here. The next day I empty a spoonful of medicine into her mouth. She shakes her head to dispel the bitter taste and then says:

— So I might really be very sick without anyone knowing!

When she sees that I am determined to keep quiet, she throws me an angry look and says:

—Why don't you answer?

With a sigh, I reply:

—What can I say to a woman who wants to make herself sick in spite of everything?

— Didn't you hear the man with your own ears?

—Yes, I heard him. Of course it's possible that a machine or two could be wrong. But I can't believe that all of them would make the same mistake at the same time!

Picking a fight, she says:

— Unbelievable? Why? It could happen!

She drops it til the next day, and then says in an unusually sweet voice:

—Would you answer me something frankly?

My heart skips a beat between my ribs, since I

know very well what that question will be. She goes on, smiling:

— But no getting angry.

In despair, I said:

— God forbid.

She hesitates a moment, collecting her courage and says:

— Would you be angry with me if I took a trip and was away for two or three weeks?

Then she adds with quickly increasing confidence:

— Really angry, I mean?

Knowing the answer, I ask:

— Take a trip where?

— Who have I got to visit besides my Hamada?

She explains to me that she has the plane ticket, that her room and board will be with Hamada (I hope there is a nutritional equivalent to *fuul* beans and *ta'miyya** in America), and that to cover her medical expenses she will sell two of her bracelets and a few bangles she'll never miss that were languishing uselessly at the bottom of her closet.

---

*Simmered whole fava beans (a mild but garlicky dish on the order of Mexican refried beans) and fried fava bean patties (known in the Levant as felafel), the two major Egyptian staples.

— I swear, if I weren't worried about you I wouldn't even wait til tomorrow! I'll see what those machines they've got over there have to say and set my mind at ease.

I remember that psychologist who accused me of wishing for her death because of my excessive worry about her. What would he say today if he saw me doing the opposite? Should I dismiss her illness so lightly, refuse her a trip for treatment she wants, even if I know it won't do any good?

I say with a mixture of sincerity and resignation:

— Don't you worry about me, Amina, go ahead and take your trip if that's what you want.

And in the silent bedroom, for the first time in many years, I find myself alone, like a frightened little boy. I imagine that the smile that was wrestling with the features in Ibrahim's picture on the wall has won after all. Between sleep and waking the lost boy's voice comes to me:

— Dad, why are you mad that Mom's coming to me?

Astonished, I say to him:

— Who told you she's coming to you?

— Didn't she take a plane this morning?

—Yes, but she's not coming to you, she's going to your brother in America. So the people where you are take planes, do they?

—I didn't say that!

—What did you say then?

—Nothing at all!

Then he smiles at me, showing gleaming white teeth in the midst of a face that suddenly turns into a black lump of charcoal.

—Aawww! Aawww! Aawww!

Suddenly a deep voice blots out the sound of the grasshoppers, a frog's voice that I hope is my friend Froggie. Immediately, all the other frogs follow him and join in singing in this open party. Their deep cavernous voices are the perfect backdrop for the chirping of the grasshopper. I hope that the pond the frogs have found has been made by a broken water pipe and not the overflow of a sewer, even though it's far-fetched, of course, to think that their voices would be affected by the type of environment from which they issue.

This ruckus, they claim, is the call of the males to the females to seduce them, which, if true, is a sign that the female frog's taste is a little strange. In any case, as we expand our application of Freudian ideas in the human race, it behooves us to be sparing in forcing them on respectable other species such as that of the frog.

—— Krrrrr! Krrrrrr! Krrrrrr!

Isis's ally salutes you, Amina, She is praying a heartfelt prayer for you, one I think you need where you are now, amongst a people—if one is to believe their films—half of whom are thieves and highway robbers and the other half of whom run beneath an endless hail of bullets. I hope Hamada is with you when you need him to help you run, wearing the blue wool pullover you stayed up nights knitting, next to me and the heater. I wonder if we'll share another of those lovely warm evenings? And why haven't you written anything to me yet besides that brief telegram saying you'd arrived safely in Los Angeles?

——Taakh! Taakh! Taakh!

It's a sound that seems to take a long time to burrow into the depths of my mind, with all the other corpses that are buried there. Even Amina cried that day, where she sat on her bed. In a voice choked with tears, she said:

—— It's true I don't like her, but it's breaking my heart!

It was the sound of the axe blows on Rina's tall graceful trunk on that unlucky day. The chopping done, they threw a long rope around her neck to strangle her, and then began pulling on it so that she would fall where they wanted her to on the ground of the shed yard. But they miscalculated, of course. Rina was not about to fall where those criminals had told her to. She leaned according to her own desires toward the fissured yellow building, heading straight for her lifelong friend, the dusty palm. She embraced it with her branches and hugged it to her, as if she'd sworn a solemn oath not to reach the ground without it. Not an iota of opposition did the old palm make, as if it had been eagerly awaiting the happy day when it would rest its leaning trunk on the bosom of Mother Earth.

As for you, Gum'a, I'm sorry to say that I can only laugh when I try to imagine your feelings as you suddenly found yourself thrown to the ground with the two trees on top of you, one tall and graceful and formerly harmonious, with a dusty palm in her arms, its cluster of red dates scattered on the ground of the shed yard. The men went about picking them up and chewing on them as they tried to extricate you from beneath the trees.

It's an accident that Gum'a might well have died in; in fact, it's truly strange that he didn't. From this, we can understand more about graceful Rina's character, how she was not merely graceful and beautiful. No, at the same time—unlike most beauties—she was tender-hearted, as well. It's true that Gum'a would willingly have refrained from slaughtering her after their long acquaintance, but he was obliged to for the sake of his daily bread. So, instead of the harsh penalty of death, it sufficed the tender-hearted Rina to just break one of his legs, and only the left one, in an additional gesture of compassion for him.

Gum'a spent one week in the hospital, and then came out with that white plaster leg. I went to visit him in the shed yard where I found him sitting in front of the fissured house, leg outstretched. Around him were a large number of birds, pecking at the ground along with the chickens, among whom might perhaps be found that hen that always wanted to lay. From inside the house, the voice of the new baby reached me as he cried, crying that had begun its transformation into that rusty old creak, although it was not yet stuck on the word "Aah."

Touching his plastered leg, Gum'a said:

— I swear, there's something holy about you, Bey!

The expression pleased me though I didn't know what had provoked it. He went on:

—This is penance for the tree that you love! This is what I get for chopping it down!

Despite the silliness of the thought, it diffused a certain secret pleasure in me. He continued:

— And when I was going to cut it down before, the next day Shahata died! Thank God it stopped there. If you weren't kind-hearted, it would have been the end of me this time.

He will need crutches for God only knows how long, and the cheapest ones on the market cost ten pounds. He knew with his innate cunning that I would have to pay him at least half that sum to lessen the feelings of guilt that he has managed, with these words, to plant in me.

— Krrrrr! Krrrrr! Krrrrr!

There's no doubt, Muuny, that it was a nice turn you did, to allow your voice to stay with me in my loneliness. Yes, I know you would rather have been buried under Zahiira and Tamaara to be with us always, as in the old days. But I would hate for you to be constantly stepped on. I know you'll be happy over there in that safe corner next to Liifa. I feel that you, too—now please don't lie—wanted to say something.

— I know I'll die before her.

Amina always liked to say that. Thanks be to God, who has disappointed you, Amuuna. If you ask how it happened, I don't really know for sure. All I know is that I had passed through the long corridor and reached the living room on my way to the kitchen to make tea. When I happened to glance towards the heater, I found her splayed out on the old wine-colored carpet. Yes, she was splayed out, not sleeping. Muuny always knew the proper way to sleep. She would align her front and back legs and tail and rest her white chin on her black forearm, her ears perked up even in the deepest sleep. But this time, the cat was fallen there, not asleep, her limbs thrown this way and that without any attempt at order. I crept over to her for some reason I can't explain, and once again found myself face to face with that profound silence that I had experienced with His Master's Voice: the no-pulse, no-motion, absolute no-belonging to the fabric of this living world. Her jaws were open like the jaws of a crocodile, her teeth showing, her mouth a big dark cave. Impossible that she had been trying to eat something, and unlikely that she had been yowling. No explanation for it other than that she was yawning. In her tired, weak body, she felt the patter of death's cold feet, so she headed for the heater, seeking warmth, believing til the end that she could light it with her magical power, she, the goddess Basiit, the spirit of Isis, goddess of magic. There in front of the heater, she stopped for a few moments, wondering where she was and what she was doing. Then she found herself dropping to the floor in exhaustion, and fell. Calmly and haughtily, she yawned and died, alone there on the old wine-colored carpet.

Yes, I always used to like to elicit that voice by gently petting its owner's smooth black back, and by touching her throat that quivered with the vibrations of her recitations. As for now, I have no alternative but to enjoy the silence, just the silence.

From the back of the shed yard, the glow of one of the black coals of Gum'a's water pipe. I imagine him as he props it against his cast to adjust the coals and coughs. In the darkness, the stone hut is a ghost of a large tomb, in whose depths lie Gum'a and his family and the birds and the cement. Little by little, the corners become clearer and begin to stand out against a yellowing sky as that coppery body appears above its roof. It is like a meddling eye, sneaking up on its own moonstruck devotees. It's the last quarter of a big yellow Isma'iliyya melon,* yellow like the sandy banks of the irrigation ditch where he threw himself to cool off, that one who came running from the farthest corners of Sinai. No, it's a charred black lump that has stolen the yellow gleam of a ray of sun. It's frozen, barren, desolate, lifeless, with tracks between the Sea of Storms and the Sea of Shadows of the shoes of some American adventurists who landed there one day. May the machines that got to the moon be able to get to the secret of your dizziness, my darling Amouna.

— Sii tiss aawww! Sii tiss aawww! Krrrrr!

The sounds intertwine and merge, fusing into one majestic melancholy voice. Then a new voice begins to creep into the piece, shyly at first, then boldly and without restraint. Like the sound of the strings in a delirious crescendo. Like green pools pressed from

---

*The region around Isma'iliyya, a small city on the Suez Canal, is famous for its melons. Someone coming to Cairo from Sinai would be likely to pass through Isma'iliyya, an association which perhaps triggers the painful memory.

the depths of the great gushing green sea. Like a beam of light that's been frozen in space, a beam that's been passed through a crystal vessel full of cosmic wine they began aging a million light-years ago. If Amina were here, she would swear it was the voice of angels, a chorus of angels that have had come down to bless our pure little garden. That would be easier for her than to admit that this is the voice of trees which they make audible when they wish, for those of their lovers whom they wish. And I am certain that tonight Liifa has said things that got lost in the shuffle as she stood caressing with her roots the skeleton of Muuni, who is yawning for all eternity.

My ear picks up a metallic tone in the midst of all those voices. After all, what should keep the ants from joining in this processional from the depths of their dark, moist holes? And that other delicate melancholy voice, like a drop of dew or a pool of light dancing under Tamaara, creeping into the heart on a fine veil of nectar. Who else could it issue from but the little white butterfly?

And off in the distance, a trembling echo of a little laugh, neither rough nor smooth, accompanied by a prayer for me that I be endowed with a brain. Then other voices, strange ones, begin intruding on the piece and spoiling its majesty. Perhaps it would be better for me to get up and go to bed just as soon as I drain the last drop from the brown porcelain cup. Yes, I'd better get up, and quickly, before I get embroiled in a vulgar exchange with that voice that I hear coming from afar, which says to me with its insolent laugh "ha'aw ha' 'aw."

Afterword

Love and Death

Whoever would like to write about Mohammed Afifi has a field of depth and breadth from which to choose. Afifi wrote short stories with skill and artistry, fashioning them in a distinctive, experimental style. His novels, skillful and creative, encompassed both the romantic and the symbolic. He has a play to his credit, and a variety of radio programs as well. Afifi was immensely cultivated, steeped in the classics and yet intimately acquainted with the very latest intellectual, artistic, and social currents.

Still, he was known as "the satirist." His satiric writings predominated in every sphere, both what was published in newspapers and magazines, and what appeared in book form. This did not come to pass haphazardly, but was rather an outgrowth of a powerful vision that took root in the depths of his being, until it became second nature. Or rather first nature, for early on he discovered the absurd character of life and

---

This is the obituary that Naguib Mahfouz wrote for Mohammed Afifi. It was published in the leading Egyptian daily, Al-Ahram, on December 21, 1981.

society. This he never lost sight of, training his discerning eye on the natural world, social relations, human conventions, and daily life. That would have been enough to make of him as gloomy an intellectual as Abu Al-'Alaa Al-Ma'arri* or Schopenhauer or as angry a man of letters as Beckett. However, his mild-mannered, gentle, and friendly nature chose for him instead the path of satirist, expressing his innermost self through jest and joke and witticism, spreading happiness and smiles rather than sorrow and distress. In short, he joined the camp of sociability, peopled by laughing rebellious spirits like Al-Jaahiz† and

---

*Al-Ma'arri, 973–1039. Born in the northern Syrian town whose name he bears, Al-Ma'arri was blinded by smallpox in early childhood. A dedicated scholar, he traveled as far as Iraq to study with scholars at the renowned language schools there. Traumatized by the death of his mother during his absence, he later led the life of a recluse. His famed philosophical poetry expresses an overwhelmingly bleak view of life.

†Abu 'Uthmaan 'Amr ibn Bahr ibn Mahbuub, nicknamed Al-Jaahiz, died 868. Prolific Abbassid writer of enormous influence. Al-Jaahiz lived in Basra, then in Baghdad, during one of the most fertile periods of sciences and letters in the Arab east. Over the course of his long life, he wrote famously in a wide variety of fields, including rhetoric, theology, and zoology. Besides its stunning breadth and depth, Al-Jaahiz's work is prized for its wonderful satiric wit.

Al-Maazini,* Al-Rehaani† and Charlie Chaplin. These were people who were determined to climb to the pinnacle of satire, and they did so by transforming life's inanity and misery into joy and mirth, thumbing their noses at fate, dancing in the face of the void.

Satire was the core of Mohammed Afifi's life. His heart beat satire, his mind thought it, his will moved in it. It was not a suit he donned when he picked up his pen and doffed when the outside world beckoned, but rather his skin and flesh and blood. It was his style in seriousness and in jest, in joy and in sorrow. No situation was immune to his satire, but it was a vari-

---

*Ibrahim 'Abd Al-Qaadir Al-Maazini, 1889–1949. Born in Cairo, Al-Maazini left teaching translation in 1918 for journalism and politics. He, Al-Shukri, and Al-'Aqqaad formed the "Diwan Group." Al-Maazini is famous for his poetry and short stories, which were characterized by humor, satire, and subtlety of description.

†Nagiib Ilyaas Rayhaan, known as Nagiib Al-Rehaani, 1891–1949. Born in Cairo to a family of Christian Iraqi extraction, he is regarded as the greatest comic actor of the Egyptian stage and cinema of his time. Famous for his irreverent and sardonic character Kishkish Bey, he has fifty plays to his credit. Unlike many of those who followed him in the '50s and '60s, Al-Rehaani's humor was often subtle and verbal rather than broad and physical.

egated satire, one whose mood and key changed according to the circumstances. That is why we, his friends, felt that we were always in the presence of his genius, not simply when we read something he had written. It is also why he was able to raise his art to the very summits of literary achievement.

I had set out here to write about Mohammed Afifi, my friend, but I have escaped into writing about the artist, escaped to keep insistent memories at bay, to avoid losing myself in sweet reveries that are no longer sweet, in memories of light-hearted, delightful talk whose voice has been forever silenced. Never mind the past two years during which the grim disease attacked our elder statesman of satire; it never defeated his spirit. But it defeated his friends who gathered around him, watching sadly, appalled, in despair. All of their love was incapable of alleviating his pain, of giving him solace. . . .*

---

*The following excerpt of an interview with Mahfouz by Mohammed Al-Zurqaani over two years later explains why Mahfouz makes no reference to *Taraniim* in his obituary. "Mohammed Afifi wrote this book while waiting for death, having been informed by his doctors that the end was near. *Taraniim* is a book of poetic, mystical meditations, written in his signature

continued on following page

Well, my departed friend, I—and all the Harafiiish—will not say "goodbye." Instead, as was our habit at the end of every evening we spent together, we say to you "until we meet again."

---

continued from previous page

his signature satiric humor. With their spirituality and the depth of their insight into life and creation, these writings are a paragon of beauty and intuitiveness. I consider this a book of poetry, beautiful and sensitive. This is a contemplation: approaching death and awaiting it, *Taraniim* is a contemplation of the life that Afifi lived, of his experiences, and of everything around him. Mohammed Afifi used to show us, the Harafiish (Naguib Mahfouz, Ahmed Mazhar, and Adil Kamil) everything he wrote before sending it off to press. But this time he did not tell us what he was writing. We used to go visit him daily, but we knew nothing of this book." Mahfouz was Afifi's closest friend, and for the better part of thirty years, he and the other members of their circle, Al-Harafiish, spent most Thursday nights at Afifi's house. After his death, Afifi's family naturally turned to Mahfouz for his professional advice on publishing the book. The memoir dazzled Mahfouz, and he refused to change a single word. However, at the time of this death, Afifi had not decided on a title, and it was Mahfouz who chose *Taraniim fii Dhill Tamaara*.